# MURDER

## AT THE OLD COTTAGE

Irish detectives Hays and Lyons return

## DAVID PEARSON

Paperback edition published by

The Book Folks

London, 2018

© David Pearson

ISBN 978-1-9809-1448-8

www.thebookfolks.com

For Robert, who has provided so much encouragement.

# Chapter One

Mary Drinan sat uncomfortably behind the small wooden desk in the room at the back of Tolan's Pharmacy in Clifden. Mary was a large woman – too large for the desk, and too large for the small room in which she sat. It was called a private consulting room, but this was very much an exaggeration. It was more like a cupboard or a cell, with just a small window of frosted glass that had bars on the outside, a single bare light bulb, and barely room to open the door inwards.

The billet had been arranged for Mary by the Health Service Executive, who had decided in their wisdom to overhaul the Clifden Health Centre, a 1960s building located on the Galway road leading out of the town. So, this was temporary, but not nearly temporary enough for Mary's liking.

Mary was the district nurse. She had been a nurse for almost thirty years, having gone into the profession straight after school at eighteen. In those days you didn't need a degree to look after sick people, just three or four

1

years working under an impossible ward sister, or worse still, a matron.

Mary's clinics were held three mornings a week on Mondays, Wednesdays and Thursdays between 10.30 and 12 noon. Unfortunately, no one came in until well after eleven, often even half past, so she never got away on time, which annoyed her greatly. It was usually after 1 p.m. by the time she had finished seeing her last patient, or 'client' as she now had to call them, in case they might be stigmatized by use of the correct term.

In the afternoons Mary called on the sick or very elderly in the area. She responded to phone calls requesting her attendance, and had a regular schedule for the old and infirm even if they had not asked for a visit.

Clifden had a lot of older folks living round and about. There was very little employment to keep young people in the area, so after they had finished attending Clifden Community School, and had done their Leaving Certificate, most of the eighteen or nineteen-year-olds departed. Some went to university in Galway, or even further afield, well beyond the normal commuting distance. Clifden was left with mainly middle-aged people who ran the shops and bars, immigrants who worked cheaply in the summer months in the hotels and gift shops, and older people, many of whom lived alone in small, often forlorn houses dotted around the countryside.

Mary's patch stretched from Cashel and Carna, through Roundstone and Ballyconneely, past Clifden and out to Leenaun, taking in Cleggan, Renvyle and Tully Cross along the way. It was a very extensive area but thankfully sparsely populated, except during the summer months of July and August when the area became thronged with tourists. It was at this time that many of the houses, locked up for the rest of the year, showed signs of life. These were the holiday homes enjoyed by the trades and professional people of Galway and even Dublin, who could afford to escape the madness of the city for a couple of weeks of peace and tranquillity amongst the beautiful scenery of Connemara. None of these transient dwellers featured on Mary's list, for which she was eternally grateful, although being big hearted as she was, she would not have refused help to anyone who was in need should they come to her attention.

To manage this extensive territory, Mary had devised a series of route maps that she now knew by heart. Some days she would leave Clifden where she lived in a small terraced house down by the harbour, and travel south to Ballyconneely, then east to Roundstone, and then on around the small twisty but very scenic roads to Carna before heading along the N59, getting her back to Clifden around five-thirty or six in the afternoon. She had other routes going north out of Clifden towards Westport that allowed her to see her clients in that area, and her trips were arranged so that she visited each of her charges approximately once every three weeks. Fortnightly would have been better, she thought, but the pressure of the long drives and the clinics three days each week in Clifden simply did not afford her the time to increase the frequency of her visits.

On this particular day, it was a Wednesday, she remembered – as if she could ever possibly forget – her clinic finished late as usual at quarter past one, and by the time she had eaten a hearty lunch of soup, a ham sandwich made from home-baked wholemeal bread, and a generous slice of hot apple pie smothered in cream, it was two o'clock. Mary had made plans for just this situation. She had clients to see this week, but the timing would only allow her to visit two, or maybe three during the afternoon. She had that number on her list between Ballyconneely and Roundstone, so that's where she would go. One old man in particular was overdue a visit, as she hadn't seen him in the previous two weeks.

It was a pleasant enough day in Clifden that early April. There were patchy clouds in the sky, but they were very high up, and with the change in the light following the spring equinox, the place looked well, getting itself ready for the summer tourist season. Mary folded herself into her little twelve-year-old Toyota which, despite having enormous mileage on the clock, almost 200,000 miles, still carried her willingly across the boggy roads in all weathers. She had harboured thoughts of updating it, but the man who serviced the little car had said when she raised the prospect with him, "They don't make them like this anymore. If I were you, I'd keep her till she stops. There's plenty of life left in her yet." And so, Mary persisted with the little car, and it hadn't let her down.

Mary's first house call that day was to Mrs Laverty. This woman was seventy-nine years old, and in generally quite good health for her age. But like all old people, she had some issues, and Mary called regularly to see that she was OK. On these visits Mary would check her blood pressure, check the fridge to see that the woman had something to eat, and see that she was taking her medication.

Mrs Laverty's house was what was known in the district as second generation. The first generation of houses in Connemara were built in the nineteenth century, or before. They were made from stones carefully piled on top of one another, then the inside was covered in a mud with reeds in it, like a sort of rough plaster. They invariably had just two rooms, one on either side of the entrance, and a clay floor. At one end, a chimney was built, with a huge open fire that was used for heat, cooking, and boiling water. Of course, these houses had no electricity, so oil lamps and candles were used for light, and all the cooking was done on the open turf fire. The roof was always thatched, which worked quite well to keep out the strong westerly winds and driving rain during the harsh winters. Entire families had been reared in these humble properties, but few remained standing, and those that did were now generally given over to providing shelter for animals between November and April each year.

By the mid-1950s, the devastating poverty that characterized the region had begun to abate. Government grants were beginning to appear, and with the inflow of funds people began to build better houses. They didn't have the insulation that we see today, but they were built of blocks on proper foundations with slate or tiled roofs, a great improvement on what had gone before. Some of the later ones even had rudimentary central heating, using a boiler at the back of the fire in the main room to heat and circulate hot water into a few radiators. When these houses started to appear, you would often see the old abandoned house left alongside the newer one.

Noreen Laverty's house was one of these and, true to form, the old abandoned thatched cottage, now in ruins, was standing about thirty metres away on the rocky site.

Mary scrambled out of the Toyota to open the five-bar gate that separated the Laverty property from the road. She drove through, and then not wanting to leave it open behind her, struggled out again to close it. She bumped cautiously over the rocky gravel track to the front of the small cottage, and before she had struggled from the car for the third time, Noreen appeared at the front door.

Noreen insisted that Mary should have a cup of tea and a slice of freshly baked cake. This was a common practice among Mary's clients, and was, at least in part, responsible for Mary's considerable girth. She yielded, protesting, to Noreen's insistence, and while the tea and cake were being prepared, Mary checked the plastic container that was set out in segments for each of the thirty-one days in the month to see that Noreen had been taking her pills, and that there was sufficient supply to last to the end of April. As Noreen opened the fridge to get out the milk, she observed that it appeared to be reasonably well stocked.

After the tea, and a chat about current affairs, and how the government was basically useless and should be doing a lot more for the people of the west, Mary gently extricated herself, promising as always to call again before the end of the month.

Although she had a schedule to keep, Mary was always conscious that she might be the only living soul that these people set eyes on from one end of the week to the other. Many of her clients no longer drove their own cars, and the bus service on these back roads was notoriously patchy, so often they had to rely on the kindness of neighbours to get into Clifden to buy provisions, or go to the chemist. There were some organized activities laid on every few weeks or so, but this hardly amounted to a dizzy social life.

By the time Mary got to her last house call of the day, she was feeling quite exhausted, and very full of tea and cake.

Her last call on this particular route was an old timer by the name of Paddy O'Shaughnessy. Paddy, a difficult man at the best of times, lived in another second-generation cottage on the mountain side of the Clifden road, quite close to Ballyconneely. To get to the house Mary turned off at the sign for the Alcock and Brown memorial at Derrygimlagh, and followed the road for about 700 metres, before turning onto the rocky track that led down into a hollow where Paddy's house sat.

Paddy's house, like himself, was dour and weather-beaten. It had once been painted white, but the rain had washed most of the paint away, so it was now a dirty grey streaky mess. Outside was untidy too. An old rusting Ford van that hadn't gone anywhere for many years lay abandoned at the side of the house, its tyres deflated, and one of the two rear doors hanging off its hinges. Empty plastic bags blew around in the breeze, and various old bits of rusty agricultural machinery completed the picture of neglect and decay.

She knocked on the dark green front door of the house. There was no reply, which she found odd as it was just about tea time, and the Angelus, followed by the television news, avidly watched by anyone over fifty, would be coming on in a few minutes.

Mary knocked again, louder this time, and called out Paddy's name, but still there was no response.

The third time she knocked, she called out, "Mr O'Shaughnessy, are you there?" But still nothing.

She started to have an uneasy feeling. It had been over two weeks since she had been here, and anything could have happened in the meantime. Paddy wasn't in bad health, but he could easily have fallen, or had a stroke. She needed to get inside the house.

She went to the front window and, shielding her eyes from the glare of the light, peered into the darkness. Inside was too dark for her to see anything at all, but she could observe that there was no light on, nor was the television lighting up the room.

Mary went around to the back of the house, picking her way carefully through the junk, and giving the old van a wide berth. She noticed at once that the back door was ajar, not wide enough to squeeze in through, not for Mary at least, but not closed either. Mary forced the door open a bit wider. It scraped along the concrete and begrudgingly parted enough to let her in.

Mary was met with a swarm of bluebottle flies, disturbed by the noise, and the sudden brightness afforded by the open door. She was also hit with the appalling stench of rotting flesh. Paddy O'Shaughnessy was home all right. There he was sitting in the 1960s armchair with bare oak arms. He was in his usual brown suit and striped shirt with no tie, but his exposed hands and face were almost black, and his body had collapsed inwards into the chair.

# Chapter Two

When Mary got over the initial shock of finding one of her patients dead in his own house, she realised that she needed to call for help. There was no signal on her mobile phone, so she left the house again by the same route through which she had entered, got into her car, and drove back up along the rocky, uneven track to higher ground. There she was relieved to find that her phone now had three bars of reception.

\* \* \*

Sergeant Séan Mulholland was alone in the Garda station in Clifden. At twenty past six, he was getting ready to call it a day, and was collecting up the open files from his desk to lock them away for the night. He should, by rights, keep the station open till eight o'clock, but at this time of year there was little doing, so he usually closed up around six-thirty and made his way across to Cusheen's Bar for a few pints and a quiet read of the paper before heading home to his own bachelor cottage on the Sky Road.

When the phone rang, he cursed under his breath.

"Typical," he said to himself, "not a peep all day, and just when you're getting ready to go…"

"Clifden Garda," he said rather curtly as he answered the call.

"Séan, is that you?" Mary asked.

"Sure, of course it is, who else would it be? Who's calling?"

"It's Mary Drinan, Séan. Look, I'm out at Paddy O'Shaughnessy's place near the monument. God, I'm calling after finding him dead in his arm chair. It's awful. Can you send someone out?" Mary said.

They had often had to deal with unpleasant situations together as the elderly from around Clifden passed over. He had a healthy respect for the woman who dealt with such matters professionally, while expressing genuine sympathy and compassion for any relatives remaining.

"God, Mary, that's dreadful. I'm on my own here today, but I'll come out myself. Has he been gone long, do you think?"

"I'm afraid he has. He's not in good shape at all, and it's partly my fault. I should have called in on him last week, but I was too busy," she said, becoming a little tearful.

"Now don't say that, Mary," Mulholland said, "wasn't he eighty or more? His time had come. Look, I'll give the ambulance a call and we'll be out as soon as we can. Oh, and, Mary, don't go back into the house. Wait till we get there."

Mulholland called the ambulance station which was just down the road and spoke to the man on duty. He arranged for an ambulance to follow him out to Paddy

O'Shaughnessy's house, adding that there was no need to rush. Paddy was beyond medical help at this stage.

Mulholland drove his black Saab on out past the secondary school and past the narrow bridge where the smoked salmon factory stood, on his way to Ballyconneely. The ambulance followed closely behind, its blue lights off. As they approached the sharp left-hand turn for the Alcock and Brown Memorial, Mulholland pulled over and waved the ambulance on, knowing that there wouldn't be a lot of room in front of O'Shaughnessy's house, and the ambulance would need to get in close to remove the body.

Mulholland pulled in behind the ambulance and got out of his car. He walked over to where Mary Drinan was standing.

"Hello Mary. God, this is sad. Are you OK?" asked Mulholland, putting on his peaked cap so that he felt more official.

"Hello Séan. He's in a bad way, poor soul. Do you mind if I don't go back in?"

"No, you're grand. You stay here. We'll see what's to be done," Mulholland said, telling the two paramedics to go inside by the back door.

\* \* \*

Inside the cottage, which was still decidedly whiffy, the two paramedics examined the remains of Paddy O'Shaughnessy, while Mulholland looked around the parlour. He saw that the television wasn't switched on, and made a mental note to ask Mary if she had turned it off when she arrived, and if she had moved the remote control from Paddy's chair to the kitchen table where it now rested.

"Jesus!" exclaimed one of the paramedics loudly, recoiling from the lifeless form of the dead man.

"Oh my God," the other said.

"What's wrong with ye?" Mulholland asked. "Have ye not seen a dead body before?"

"You'd better come and see for yourself, Sergeant," the older of the two said.

Séan Mulholland was not one for dead bodies, especially if they had been dead a while and were partly decomposed. Nevertheless, he crossed the room and bent down to where the ambulance man was pointing with his pen.

"Look here," he said, "and here," pointing to Paddy O'Shaughnessy's emaciated wrists. "He's been tied to the chair with plastic tie wraps. And his ankles are the same, they're bound to the front chair legs. This poor old man didn't die peacefully in front of the fire, that's for sure!" the paramedic said.

"Good God in heaven!" Mulholland exclaimed. "Don't touch him now. You can't move him. I don't know what's happened here, but I'll have to get help. Can you stay a while if I go and call this in to Galway?"

"We can, but not long. We're on duty, and there's only Séamus back at the station, and we could be needed."

"I'll be as quick as I can. Be sure not to touch anything. Best you wait in the ambulance, if that's OK?" Mulholland said, leaving by the stiff back door to drive up to the road where his mobile phone would work.

Outside, Mary was standing by his car.

"Look, Mary, this isn't straightforward, I'm afraid. I'm sorry to tell you this, but the paramedics discovered that

Paddy had been bound to his chair," he said, shaking his head as if he couldn't quite believe it himself.

"Bound. How do you mean?" she asked, frowning.

"There are plastic cable ties around his wrists and ankles. I don't think Paddy just passed away. There's more to it. I'll have to call in the team from Galway now. Can you bide a while till they get here? They'll need to get your statement."

"Dear God in heaven, what happened to the poor man? I don't understand," Mary said, her eyes now filled with tears that ran down her cheeks.

"Neither do I, but we'll get to the bottom of it, don't worry. And you have nothing to blame yourself for, it's not your doing. I'll be back in a few minutes, I have to call Galway now. Sit in, if you like."

Mary sat in Mulholland's car. She didn't want to be left alone with her thoughts at this terrible time, and of course she felt guilty – so very guilty.

# Chapter Three

Inspector Mick Hays was almost home when his mobile phone began to ring. He had it linked by Bluetooth to his car's music system, so he was able to answer it hands free.

He had left Galway Garda station about twenty minutes previously having spent quite a boring day catching up on emails and paperwork following his recent week off.

Hays had a brother who lived and worked in Horsham in the south of England. He had gone to England in the 1980s when Ireland was in the grip of one of its regular recessions. With a good degree from Galway University, he had found work easily in the United Kingdom, and was now a senior manager in Royal Sun Alliance, the biggest employer in the town. Along the way he had met and married Sara, a lovely English rose, and they now had two children, a boy and a girl, the classic British nuclear family.

Hays had spent a very enjoyable week as their guest. His brother Aidan had taken the week off too, and the group had spent the time travelling around the south of England, visiting Brighton, Arundel Castle, Glynde Palace, Chartwell, the family home of Winston Churchill, and of course some of the finest pubs and restaurants that England could offer. The weather had been kind, as it often is in this part of England, and Hays had thoroughly enjoyed the week, leaving behind the pressure of the job and catching up on old times with Aidan over pints of locally brewed craft beer in the Dog and Bacon, conveniently located just at the end of Collingwood Road where Aidan's four bedroomed detached house was to be found.

Hays' Bluetooth set-up identified the caller as Séan Mulholland, so he knew at once that something serious was up.

"Hello Séan. What can I do for you on this fine spring evening?"

"Mick? We have a situation out here near Clifden." Mulholland went on to describe what he termed a 'suspicious death'. Having heard the details, Hays had to agree that it certainly sounded suspicious, and told the sergeant that he was on his way, and not to let anyone touch anything till he arrived.

Swinging the car around, Hays put on his blue lights and siren, in an attempt to scythe his way through the notorious evening traffic in Galway, and headed west.

As he raced down the back streets bordering the Shantalla area, and intercepted the Séamus Quirke Road heading for Newcastle and the N59, he made several calls on the phone.

The first was to Detective Sergeant Maureen Lyons, his very able, if somewhat cheeky, assistant in the Galway

Detective Unit. Lyons didn't answer, so when it went to voicemail, he left a short but unambiguous message, "Maureen, call me when you get this."

The second call was to Doctor Julian Dodd, the pathologist attached to Galway Regional Hospital. Here he had more luck, though it's fair to say Dodd wasn't exactly delighted to hear from Hays. He rarely called with good news. He asked Dodd to meet him out at O'Shaughnessy's house as soon as possible, and for once Dodd didn't complain, as Wednesday was his wife's bridge night and he would have nothing better to do in any case.

The sirens and blue flashing lights did quite a good job of parting the traffic in front of him, until that is, he reached Moycullen. There was a steady stream of traffic coming against him, and an old lady in a Nissan Micra in front of him who steadfastly refused to let him pass. He flashed his lights and blew the horn, but still she wouldn't budge, until eventually she turned off to the left allowing Hays to pick up speed again.

His third phone call had been to Detective Garda Eamon Flynn. As he couldn't reach Lyons, he would have to settle for Flynn as his bagman on this occasion. Flynn was still in the station and was quite pleased to get a call from the boss telling him to attend the scene of a suspicious death, even if it was in the back of beyond.

By seven-thirty the entire entourage had turned up and poor Paddy O'Shaughnessy's property was festooned with vehicles as it had never been before.

Hays gathered the group together. He firstly asked Flynn to take a statement from the nurse, and then let her away home, as she was clearly distressed. Before he dispatched her, he asked if the dead man had any relatives living in the area, but Mary knew of none. Next, he asked Mulholland to get a statement from the senior ambulance crew member. Meanwhile Hays himself, the pathologist, and the other ambulance man, all wearing plastic gloves, white paper scene of crime suits, and carrying a body bag, went back into the house.

The first thing that Hays did was to go and open the front door so that access to the house could be made easier.

The doctor and the ambulance man focused on the body of the old man. Dodd examined the head, hands, ankles and all of the exposed blackening skin. Before anything was allowed to be disturbed, Hays took dozens of photographs on his mobile phone, the flash of the camera lighting up the inside of the house momentarily with an eerie blue-white light as each frame was captured.

As he moved around the house, Hays could see that the place appeared to have been thoroughly searched. It was not ransacked, in fact far from it. But Hays could see that the patterns of dust that an open turf fire inevitably leaves in a small house, had been disturbed. Books had distinct ash lines contrasting with clean areas; jam jars had been moved, leaving a circle of clean surface where they had previously been placed. Hays concluded that the whole house had been thoroughly gone over, but not in a reckless way.

Eventually, the doctor signalled to the paramedics to cut the tie wraps away, putting them into an evidence bag.

Moving carefully, the body of Paddy O'Shaughnessy was gently lowered into a body bag, which by now was sitting on a light weight stretcher. The black plastic bag was zipped up, and the second paramedic was summoned to carry the load out of the house and into the ambulance. A few minutes later the bright yellow and green vehicle left the site, swaying and bouncing back up the rocky track, heading for the mortuary in Galway.

"Any initial observations, Doc?" Hays asked Dodd.

"A few. But I'm not saying much till I've examined the body thoroughly tomorrow," the doctor responded.

"What can you say then?" said Hays, a little impatiently.

"I can say that the man was quite badly treated as he sat tethered in his favourite armchair. He's been hit around the head quite badly, and there appear to be cigarette burns on the back of his hands," the doctor reported.

"So, it's a racing certainty that he didn't die of natural causes then," Hays said.

"Sometimes, Inspector, your powers of detection amaze me. I can't disagree with you on that one, unless you can show me how a man can bind his arms and legs to a chair, and then hit himself repeatedly around the head and apply a lighted cigarette to the back of his hands. Oh, and by the way, he wasn't a smoker," he added.

"No, I gathered that. There's no sign of any smoking material round and about."

"What about time of death?" Hays said.

The doctor gave Hays a sardonic look before saying, "Sometime between the last time he was seen alive and today, I imagine."

"Just asking, Doc, just asking."

Outside the house, Flynn had finished taking statements, and had asked the ambulance men to come in to the Garda station in Clifden the following morning to read and sign them.

With the body of Paddy O'Shaughnessy now on its way to Galway, Julian Dodd packed up the few tools of his gruesome trade, removed his vinyl gloves, and prepared to leave.

"Ten o'clock tomorrow OK then for the preliminary PM?" he asked Hays.

"Could you leave it till two o'clock, Doctor? I'll need to come back out here in the morning for an hour or so with the forensic team, but I should be back in the city by two."

"Fine, two o'clock it is, see you then," the doctor replied, heading for his car.

Hays then turned to Eamon Flynn and said, "I'm sorry to do this to you, Eamon, but I need you to stay on point overnight here. You can go into Clifden now and have something to eat, get some supplies. I'll wait here till you get back. OK?"

"Yes, OK, boss. I guess someone has to do it," Flynn replied.

Hays spent the hour that Flynn was away having a really good look around the cottage, both outside and in. There was no point looking for tyre tracks – all the vehicles that had come and gone since the nurse had found the body made sure of that.

Hays went slowly around the place, putting scenarios together in his head. How many assailants had assisted Paddy on his way to the next world? What could possibly be the motive for killing an old, solitary man in this way? What was being searched for in the house while Paddy sat immobilized in his favourite armchair?

When Flynn returned he was well provisioned with a wrapped sandwich, two chocolate bars, and a large bottle of Ballygowan fizzy water.

"Breakfast," he simply said when he observed Hays casting an eye over his supplies.

"What time do you reckon you'll get here in the morning, boss?" Flynn asked.

"Early. I'll try and get the boys moving by eight, so we should be here around nine. Before you settle down for the night of undisturbed slumber in the comfort of your car, make sure to secure the house and put lots of tape up, won't you?" Hays instructed.

"I can't stay in there then, boss?"

"No, 'fraid not. We can't afford any more contamination of the scene before the forensic boys have a good go over it. This looks like a pretty nasty murder to me."

Hays said goodnight to the young detective and drove back up the rocky track towards the road. The light was fading fast now, and he put on his headlights, but still managed to catch the underside of his car on some protruding rocks.

As he approached the road on higher ground his phone beeped several times. At the top of the track Hays pulled the car over. He had two missed calls from Maureen Lyons, one timed at just after 8 p.m. and a second one just a few minutes ago.

Hays rang Maureen back.

"Hi boss," she said, "I've been trying to call you. What's up?"

"I had no signal there for a while," he replied. "I'm out at Derrygimlagh, near Clifden for a change. It's a long story. Would you mind if I called in when I get back to town? I don't want to say too much over the phone."

"Sounds intriguing. Sure, drop in. How long do you reckon you'll be?" she asked.

"About an hour and a half or so. See you then," he said, and hung up.

# Chapter Four

When Mick Hays had left the scene, Flynn did his best to get comfortable for the night. He sat into the passenger's seat of his car and reclined it as far as it would go in an attempt to lie out flat. He turned on the radio but discovered that the only station that he could pick up in this location was BBC Radio Four on long wave. It was in the middle of a news programme blathering on about British politics in which Flynn had no interest whatever. Try as he might to get something he could actually listen to, nothing came through.

A steady south westerly wind was blowing in from the Atlantic across Connemara that night. The wind had scooped up tons of water vapour as it crossed the sea, and as soon as it found landfall, the ground pushed up the clouds to the point where the water vapour condensed into rain, which fell back upon the land in fierce waves, driven by the brisk wind.

In Flynn's car, the rain sounded like small pebbles hitting the roof, the windscreen and the side windows.

And of course, as the rain fell it cooled the air, so it wasn't long before Flynn began to feel decidedly chilly.

"Feck this," he said to himself.

He got out of the car and ran with his torch to the back of the cottage, squeezing through the back door which scraped across the flags as he pushed it further open.

Using his torch, he entered the old man's bedroom. The room was small, and very sparsely furnished. The bed, an old iron and brass number straight out of the 1950s, occupied the centre of the room with its head to the side wall of the cottage. To Flynn's right was a small brown wardrobe with a mirrored door. Beside the bed was a brown wooden night stand with an opening that made a shelf just under the top, and a small door that made the lower part into a cupboard. The top of the night stand was badly stained with cup rings where wet or hot cups had been placed upon it over the years.

The bed was made. It appeared that the duvet had not arrived in Paddy O'Shaughnessy's lifestyle as yet, for the bed was covered in an old wine-coloured eiderdown, beneath which two heavy woollen blankets made up the rest of the arrangement. A pair of cotton sheets, quite grey in colour, and a well-used single pillow completed the picture.

The eiderdown was too small to be of any use to Flynn, so putting his torch down on the night stand, he started to pull the top blanket off the bed. The bed had been well made, and the blanket was tucked in tightly under the thin horse-hair mattress. Flynn heaved at the cream-coloured blanket and managed to pull it free. As he did so, a small sheaf of papers came out from under the mattress and fell face down at his feet.

Flynn bent down to pick up the papers but stopped himself before he had touched anything. He felt it better not to contaminate the scene any further, in case it might interfere with evidence that would be needed later. He gathered the blanket up in his arms, collected his torch and dashed back through the driving rain to his car.

Flynn settled into a most uncomfortable night's sleep. He had tucked the blanket in around his body as best he could, but had kept it well away from his face, as the blanket frankly didn't smell too good. Eventually the rain eased off, and the wind died down to a murmur. At around two o'clock the moon appeared casting an eerie light on the surroundings. Flynn finally fell into a restless sleep.

It was just around five in the morning when Flynn's nightmare started. He dreamt he was in a huge field of golden wheat. But the crop had caught fire, and the flames were now advancing in his direction. He ran for his life, but no matter how hard he ran, the smoke and flames were getting closer, and he felt he would surely be roasted alive. Just before the flames, now raging high up into the clouds and blocking out the sun, caught him, there were two loud cracks that woke him, terrified, from the dream.

What Flynn saw when he shook himself awake put the fear of God into him. Not thirty metres away, O'Shaughnessy's cottage was ablaze. Smoke and flames poured from the two windows either side of the front door. The door itself was blistering in the heat, with flames starting to lick underneath it. The slated roof had caught too, sagging dangerously at the end over the parlour.

"Jesus Christ," he shouted to no one, "what the fuck is going on?"

He disentangled himself from the blanket which seemed to have encapsulated his entire body, and struggled out of the passenger's side door. Pushed back by the smoke and heat coming from the burning house, he ran around the back of the car and got in the driver's side. He started the car and reversed at speed until he was a safe distance away from the inferno. He tried his mobile phone, but of course there was no signal, so, in a fury, he drove the car back up the rocky track till he found two bars of reception.

Clifden fire brigade sprang into action when they received Flynn's 999 call. The night man summoned a crew of four, and within half an hour they had arrived at the cottage which by now had largely burnt itself out. The four walls still stood, and some of the roof trusses, now blackened, charred and smouldering, were still holding on. Largely it was mostly the pale blue smoke of charcoal and a few stubborn pockets of flame that met the crew as they used the tank in the fire tender to douse what was left of the house.

"I thought you were supposed to be watching the place," said the lead fireman to Flynn. Flynn replied rather sheepishly, "Don't you start. I'm in enough trouble as it is. Any idea what started it?"

"Not sure. You weren't by any chance sitting by the fire in there and fell asleep, were you?" the fireman asked.

"No, I bloody wasn't! I was in the fecking car. In there's a crime scene – or was more like it."

"One of the lads says he thought he got a whiff of petrol round near the back door, but we'd need to do a proper examination to be sure when it's all cooled down."

"There's a full Garda forensic team due out here at nine o'clock. They'll find whatever caused it, I'm sure," Flynn said.

"One less job for us to do. I'll start packing up. Are you going to call this in then?" the fireman asked.

"Jaysus, I'm not looking forward to that," Flynn replied, walking back towards his car.

# Chapter Five

Hays arrived at Maureen Lyons' house down by the river in Galway at just after ten-thirty. The drive in from Connemara was tiring, and at various stages he had to slow right down, the visibility was so poor. Hays was conscious that there were often sheep loose on the road out that way, and if you hit one with your car, it led to hours of delay while you went off to find the owner and then haggled over the price of the beast. Most people wouldn't bother, but Hays wasn't like that.

Lyons let him in on the first ring of the doorbell. She lived in a small terraced house that had been divided into two flats, and hers was on the upper floor. Although it was small, with the kitchen, diner and lounge all in one room to the front, Maureen had it nicely done out.

"God, you look worn out," she said when he had taken off his coat and settled on the sofa.

"Can I get you something?"

"A drop of whiskey would be great, if you have it," he said.

"Sure, water, ice?"

"No, just as it comes. Thanks."

Hays explained the events of the evening in as much detail as he could remember. Lyons apologized for not being able to take his calls. One of the civilian workers from the station was leaving to go on a world hiking tour with her boyfriend, and a few of the people from the office had gone to Doherty's after work to give her a send-off.

Hays reassured her that there was no need to apologize, and finished the story. They both got some amusement from the fact that their colleague Eamon Flynn had been left out in Derrygimlagh to guard the house.

When Hays had finished relating the events of the evening, he asked Lyons, "Any initial thoughts?"

"It's a difficult one. I can't see what anyone would have to gain from killing an old guy like that. And it's not exactly an easy place to find, so I'm sorry, so far nothing springs to mind."

They talked on for a while longer. The whiskey and the long day had started to get to Hays, prompting Lyons to say, "You look exhausted. You'd better stay over, don't you think?"

"Thanks, I'd like that, but I'm afraid it will just be company tonight. I'm all in."

"But of course," she said, smiling, and winking at her boss.

* * *

Hays' iPhone started jumping up and down on the night stand on his side of Maureen's double bed. Hays woke, and picked up the phone, seeing that it was five forty-five am, and the caller was none other than the beleaguered night watchman, Eamon Flynn.

"Yes, Eamon, what the fuck is wrong?" he croaked into the phone.

"Jesus, boss, it's bad. The fecking place is burnt to the ground." Flynn went on to describe the events of the past hour that had seen Paddy O'Shaughnessy's house reduced to ashes.

Hays was out of the bed now, scrambling for his underpants as he continued to listen and talk to Eamon Flynn.

"Stay there. I'll be out as soon as I can, and I'll try to get Sergeant Lyons out too. Can you make sure the firemen are still there? I'll need to talk to them. Oh, and Eamon, are you OK?"

By this time Maureen Lyons had tuned in to the conversation, and was putting on her own clothes in a hurry.

* * *

As they drove out at speed with no traffic at all at that early hour, the daylight was breaking through.

"What do you make of it?" Hays asked as they passed Moycullen.

"Hard to say till we see the place. This whole thing is kinda weird. I mean what could an old guy like that have that was worth killing him for? And how the hell did it burn down, unless Flynn was playing silly buggers with a box of matches!"

"I don't think so. He said he was asleep in the car when the fire broke out, and I'm inclined to believe him."

When they reached Derrygimlagh they could hardly believe what they saw. What had been a rather modest and run-down cottage was now gone. Instead, four grey walls streaked with soot stood with charred rafters reaching upwards towards the early morning sky. The smell of burning pervaded the air, and pools of dirty black sooty water lay around where the fire crew had sprayed the burning hulk. Flynn's car was parked about twenty-five metres away from the house, and a red Volkswagen Passat with FIRE written in large white letters on the door was standing nearby.

Hays stopped their car and they both got out.

"Jesus, Eamon, what a mess. How the hell did this happen?"

Flynn went back over the story, including where he went into the house and took the blanket from the old man's bed, and how some papers had fallen on the floor. Hays felt that Flynn's story was genuine, although he was still shocked at how this could have happened with him parked just feet away.

Lyons had introduced herself to the fire officer who told her his name was Paul Staveley. He explained that they had to send the fire tender back to Clifden in case it was needed, but he could stay on for a while if he could be of any help. He walked Lyons to the back of the old house and pointed to what was left of the back door – basically a couple of charred boards hanging off their hinges.

"I'm fairly certain it was arson," Staveley said, "there are some patches of what I believe to be petrol here and there, and there's some more spilled on the grass going up the bank behind the house."

"How certain can you be?"

"I've seen enough of these in my time, Sergeant. Of course, your forensic team will be able to confirm it when they get here."

On the way out in the car, Lyons had called the station in Galway and asked that the forensic team be hurried along, given the new situation. She was assured that they would be mobilized as soon as possible, and would be there before 9 a.m.

Hays was still talking to Eamon Flynn.

"Do you need to go home and get some sleep?" he asked.

"No. I couldn't sleep now anyway. What do you need me to do, boss?" Flynn replied.

"OK. This whole thing is a mess. There's more to it than it looks. Can you get yourself into Clifden? Get some breakfast, and then get Mulholland out of bed. Ask him to lend us Jim Dolan. Then I want the two of you to comb out every shop, pub, chemist, and as many private houses as you can cover. I want to build a profile of Paddy O'Shaughnessy. And then get your arse back into Galway for a full briefing at five o'clock. OK?"

Lyons got contact details for Paul Staveley, thanked him for his input, and for waiting till they got there, and said he could go. Then the two detectives got back into Hays' car.

"The fire guy reckons it was definitely arson. He says there are traces of petrol on the grass behind the house, and in the house near the back door. He seems to think the arsonists came down the bank at the back, and they spilled some as they approached. Even if Eamon had been awake, he probably wouldn't have seen them."

"OK. Let's drive up to the monument and see if we can find out how they got here."

Hays drove back up the rocky track to the road, and instead of turning right, he turned left up towards the monument itself. The road looped around to the left, and soon they found that they were looking down on the back of O'Shaughnessy's house from above. Hays stopped the car in the middle of the road and got out.

"If I was using this approach to the house, I'd pull my car well in to the side of the road just about twenty metres on from here in case another vehicle came past," Hays said.

"Let's see if we can see any traces at the side of the road. I think I can see where the grass has been trodden on leading down to the house. Stay on the road though, we don't want to contaminate any evidence."

The edge of the road was covered in loose limestone chips, and then it bled away into the tufty, boggy grass and reeds. There was no kerb as such, and it was clear to see that there had indeed been a vehicle here recently, and that it had left tracks in the mud.

"When forensics get here, bring them up to look at this. In the meantime, I'll tape off the road," Hays said.

The forensic folks arrived on time at nine o'clock. There were three of them, led by a short girl with shoulder-length mousey-coloured hair, tied back in a ponytail.

"Hi Sinéad. Sorry to interrupt your beauty sleep, but we've got a right puzzle on here for you," Hays said to her as she climbed down out of the unmarked 4x4.

"Nothing new there then! Why can't you arrange these crime scenes a bit nearer the city, Mick? You know

I'm allergic to fresh air, and where's the nearest coffee shop?" Sinéad quipped.

"That's OK then. The whole place stinks anyway, so you should feel quite at home! How many white suits have you got with you?"

"Just the three of us. If you wake any more of them up at dawn, they spontaneously combust!"

"Ouch!"

"Sorry, bad joke."

"Can you get someone up on the road behind the house? There's some possible tyre tracks up there and maybe more. Maureen will show you the exact spot," Hays said.

"Trying to take my job now are ye, ye blaggard, Mick Hays? OK. I'll get Simon onto that. He's good with rubber!" Sinéad smirked.

The forensic team, all suited up in white paper suits with face masks, started to work on the site. They bagged up small morsels of potential evidence from both outside and inside the house.

Lyons had gone off with Simon to deal with the tyre tracks further up the road when Sinéad came over to Hays who was standing off, leaning against his car. She was holding out a plastic evidence bag with some singed pieces of white paper inside.

"You might want to have a look at these," she said, holding it out in front of her. "Don't open it, but you can see through the bag there's the corner off what looks like a bank statement, and some kind of advertising pamphlet. They're badly singed, but we may be able to get something off them."

"Nice. Can I keep them?" he asked.

"For the moment, but if you're handling it use plastic gloves, there may be still something useful on the paper."

At half-past ten, with the forensic team going about their painstaking, methodical work, Hays and Lyons set off again for Galway. As neither of them had had any breakfast, they were both famished, and stopped at Keogh's in Ballyconneely for a cooked breakfast and lots of coffee. As they sat there over their second cup, Hays said, "When we get back to Mill Street, can you see about setting up an incident room? Dodd is doing the PM on the old guy at two o'clock. See if you can delegate so you can come along."

"Sure, boss," Lyons replied.

"Oh, and set up a team briefing for five o'clock too," he added.

There was still very little traffic about as they drove back through Oughterard and Moycullen. The Newcastle road was slow as usual, but they were back at the station by midday, and Lyons set about organizing the incident room on the third floor of the station.

There were currently rumours circulating that the government had approved the construction of a new regional headquarters for Galway that would house the major crime teams and an armed response unit, as well as the main detective unit, leaving Mill Street as the central public office for the city. For the moment though, all these functions were squeezed into the old 1980s building, so space was at a premium.

# Chapter Six

Doctor Julian Dodd had started work on the emaciated corpse of Paddy O'Shaughnessy when the two detectives arrived for the post mortem. The body had already been cut open in the familiar 'Y' style, and the major organs were being removed and weighed before being preserved in large glass jars.

Lyons felt distinctly queasy at the sight of the poor man who had obviously been dead for quite some time before being found by Nurse Drinan. Her unease was not helped by the strong smell of disinfectant struggling to cope with the putrefaction being given off by the body on the shiny aluminium slab. As usual, Dodd had equipped himself with two assistant pathologists, along to learn the trade and benefit from his self-appraised infinite wisdom.

"No doubt you want me to solve the case for you as usual, Mick?" Dodd said as he moved around the table, followed eagerly by a female student who was much too interested in the proceedings for Hays' liking.

"Just tell us what you know, Doc. We'll let you solve it for us later," Hays replied.

"A gentleman in his late seventies or early eighties. Generally in good health, apart from the obvious. Meagrely but fairly well nourished with good muscle tone for his age. I'd say he walked a good bit. No sign of any serious arthritis which is unusual given his living conditions; a non-smoker, or at least he hasn't smoked for over twenty years. He took a drink, but not to excess. His liver is, or was, in good order," Dodd said in a slightly haughty manner. "Now to the bits that will interest you two. He died about ten days ago. It's terribly difficult to be any way accurate in these cases. But I've looked at the ambient day and night temperatures for the area for the last two weeks, and plotted these against the degree of decay, and give or take a day or two either way, I'd say ten days is about right.

"Initially I thought he had just passed away, but that's not the case. There's blunt force trauma damage to the left side of his head that caused quite a severe internal bleed. I'd say the poor old man died from a stroke a few minutes after that was administered, it was pretty forceful.

"Oh, and as you know, his hands and feet were bound to the chair where he was found. Apart from being very unusual, we can tell a little from the bindings that were still present."

Dodd signalled to the junior assistant, a young female student with surprisingly ruddy cheeks given the circumstances. The girl went to the side table and brought forward a plastic evidence bag containing four plastic tie wraps. She gave the bag to Lyons.

"I suppose they just look like any old tie wraps to you, Maureen," Dodd said, teasing the sergeant, "but they're not. These are branded ones, and for once they're not from China. These were made in the USA and are a brand favoured by those who dabble in computers, or should I say I.T. as we're supposed to call it these days," Dodd said.

"Any particular type of computer?" she asked.

"I haven't a clue. That's what we employ detectives for, so over to you on that one," he replied. The young assistant couldn't help but stifle a giggle at the way Dodd had dismissed the woman. She had been dismissed in the same way many times by the good doctor and was glad that his sarcasm had been sent in a different direction on this occasion.

"Anything further, Doc?" Hays asked.

"Nothing more for now. There's no prints on the tie wraps, or any DNA that is useable. I'll file them under 'G' for gruesome murders," he said. "I'll have a full report to you by tomorrow evening." He returned to his unenviable task, the Dr Dodd show being over for the moment.

Hays and Lyons left the pathology suite glad that they hadn't had a big lunch before the post mortem.

"What I can't figure out is 'why'?" he said. "What's the motive? In these cases of remote solo dwellers being assaulted, it's nearly always robbery. But this poor devil didn't seem to have anything worth taking, not that we know of anyway."

"He might have had a pile of cash hidden in a biscuit tin, I suppose," Lyons said.

"I doubt it. And if so, where's the tin? They never take it with them. Plus, he had thirty euro in his trouser pocket. If robbery was the motive, that would have gone too," Hays said.

"And it's not as if you'd just happen across that house either. It can't be seen from the main road. Someone must have known it was there and targeted it deliberately," Lyons said.

"Let's get back and see what we can find out about Paddy O'Shaughnessy."

# Chapter Seven

At five o'clock, the team assembled in room 310 where Lyons had arranged for an incident room to be set up. It wasn't spacious, but all the essentials were there. A large whiteboard on casters dominated the space between the two windows. There were two desks, one against each wall left and right, each with a PC and a telephone, and the remaining space in the middle of the floor had a further three chairs that had frankly seen better days. They were wooden, upholstered in a kind of sickly green tweed fabric, now stained and frayed at the edge of the seats.

The team consisted of Hays, Lyons, Flynn and a young uniformed Garda, John O'Connor, whom Hays had found useful in the case of the murdered Polish girl the previous year. This time they had been assigned a civilian as well to keep the paperwork in order. Sally Fahy was a bright young girl with blonde hair that she wore in a bob. She had worked with the Gardaí for over a year, and had earned a reputation for great thoroughness and order when collating and arranging files. In truth, she had made herself indispensable.

"Right. Let's get started everyone, or we'll be here all night," Hays said.

"Again," mumbled Flynn.

"Yes, all right, Eamon. Your medal is in the post," Hays quipped to a murmur of subdued laughter.

Turning to the whiteboard, Hays pointed to the picture of the deceased.

"Paddy O'Shaughnessy, at eighty-one, killed in his own home in Derrygimlagh near Clifden following a beating and more. We know very little about the man at this stage, unless Eamon has discovered that he won the Lotto or something. Eamon?"

Flynn stood up. "I've been all round Clifden today with Jim Dolan from the station out there. Before I came back in, Jim and I compared notes, and I'll summarize what we now know," he said.

"O'Shaughnessy was a very private sort of person. He had a few acquaintances in King's Bar in the town, but only to have the odd pint with. Seems he returned to Clifden about eight years ago after his mother passed away and left him the house. We called to both banks in the town, but couldn't find an account in his name. Nothing at the Post Office either which means that his pension must be paid directly into some bank account somewhere. We were told that he used to drive the white van until about two years ago, but since then he'd used the bus to come and go, or got lifts."

"Did you speak to the nurse?" Hays asked.

"No. She must have been out doing her house calls, boss."

"I'll talk to Sergeant Lyons about that after the briefing. When I was out at the cottage this morning, the forensic girl gave me a small bag of some paper fragments that weren't totally destroyed in the fire. John, I hope you're good at jigsaw puzzles. Tomorrow, I want you to see if you can get any useful information from the scraps of paper. Sally, can you give him a hand?" Hays asked.

"Well, yes, sir, I suppose so, but you know I'm not really supposed to handle evidence or anything like that," she said. She was always willing to help out with whatever was going on but was very conscious of the boundaries laid down for civilian workers in the force.

"I know that, Sally, but this is an all hands situation. I'll cover you for any flack that arises," Hays replied.

Hays went on to brief the team on the discovery of vehicle tracks and petrol at the cottage, and Doctor Dodd's discovery of the provenance of the tie wraps.

When he had finished his summing up, he said to Flynn, "You'd better go home and get a good night's sleep, Eamon. You're off till eleven tomorrow, then I might want you to go back to Doctor Dodd and pester him for anything else you can get from him. Maureen, can you stay back for a few minutes please. We'll have another briefing tomorrow at five unless there are any major developments," he said, dismissing them for the night.

* * *

Back in his office with Maureen Lyons, Hays was not happy.

"It's an awful shame Eamon didn't get to talk to the nurse," he grumbled.

"Can you go out there first thing and track her down? She probably knows more about Paddy O'Shaughnessy than anyone else. You don't get that close to a person without finding out a good deal about them. Take her to lunch. Use your female sisterhood stuff to pump her for all she knows."

Lyons strongly disliked any kind of talk that could be described as sexist. She knew Mick Hays treated her more than equally with her male colleagues, but still she bristled at his reference to her 'sisterhood stuff'. She decided though, given the humour he was in, not to react, but she would file it away for another time.

"Sure, boss, I'll get out there early and catch her before the clinic starts, see what I can get from her."

# Chapter Eight

In the world of crime detection, the police rarely get a lucky break. A detective can go through an entire career without one, and often they feel that the odds are heavily stacked in favour of the villains.

But sometimes, just occasionally, luck shines on the right side.

Maureen Lyons knew something about this. In her case, it was all about being in the right place at the right time. As a young uniformed Garda, she had been on the beat on Eyre Square in Galway one late summer morning. As she approached the Permanent TSB Bank, the door burst open, and an armed robber in a balaclava came charging out. He had a sawn-off shotgun in his right hand and a supermarket bag full of money in the other. Maureen acted with split-second timing. She stuck her foot out and tripped the fleeing thief. Not having a spare hand to break his fall, he went down on the pavement flat on his face with a sickening slap as his nose broke. The gun flew in one direction, and the cash in the other, scattering bundles of twenty euro notes in all directions. All Maureen had to do was to kneel on the robber's back and handcuff him, while of course arresting him on suspicion of armed robbery. The small crowd that had seen these goings on applauded Maureen, and even gathered up the loose cash and put it back into the bag. As Maureen said later at the press conference, "It's all about being in the right place at the right time."

* * *

At ten o'clock on the night after Hays had given the briefing, a fire engine from Galway was returning to base after a shout. The driver had come back via the docks, intending to cross the river on Father Griffin Road and get back to the station for a well-earned cup of tea.

As they made their way along the docks, one of the firemen in the back seat of the truck shouted, "STOP!" The driver braked hard bringing the heavy vehicle to an abrupt standstill.

"What is it, Brendan?" he asked.

"Back up a bit, Cathal, I saw something in that disused yard back there."

Cathal put on the blue lights and reversed the fire engine back until it was in line with the yard gate. Sure enough, a few metres inside the gate, a dark coloured BMW was starting to burn. Cathal swung the truck into the yard and stopped close to the car. Brendan grabbed the extinguisher from the cab of the fire engine, and jumped down onto the cracked concrete. The fire was in the back seat of the car, and although the seats and headlining were alight, the fire was not really established. It only took Brendan a few moments to put out the blaze, leaving nothing but black smoke issuing from the rear windows of the ill-fated vehicle.

As in all such cases, the fire had to be reported to the Gardaí. As luck would have it, Brendan the firefighter had been out on a few dates with Maureen Lyons the previous year. It hadn't come to anything, but he still had her mobile number in his phone.

* * *

Maureen was surprised to see 'Brendan' light up on the screen of her phone as she sat at home sipping a glass of red wine in front of the television. She was relieved to find that it was a work-related call. She had got on OK with Brendan, but there was no electricity between them, and his shift patterns made meeting difficult, so they had decided not to pursue things any further. In addition, Maureen had hoped that her relationship with Mick Hays might have developed a bit more quickly, although that seemed to be taking forever, if it was going to happen at all.

Maureen's instinct told her that the burning car might just be relevant to their current enquiries. It was better to be safe than sorry in any case. If it turned out to be connected, and she hadn't acted on it, then she, and all of the others on the case, would be made to look very foolish indeed.

When she had finished the call with Brendan, thankfully avoiding the 'we must meet up for a drink sometime,' a meaningless exchange in any case, Maureen called Mill Street and spoke to Sergeant Donal Walshe. She asked him to arrange for a tow truck to go down to the yard and collect the BMW, and bring it back to the station where it would be secured in the locked yard until morning.

She then phoned Hays at home and related the story to him. When she told him about Brendan, the fireman, he asked, "Should I be worried?"

"Not unless you're thinking of setting yourself on fire," she quipped, and they both laughed out loud.

"That's good work, Maureen. Even if there's no connection to O'Shaughnessy, it's still good work. We'll make a proper detective of you yet!" he joked.

"Great!" she said. "I'll start giving classes to the less gifted soon."

# Chapter Nine

It was a bright spring morning when Maureen Lyons set off from Galway heading for Clifden and her meeting with Mary Drinan. It was one of the nurse's clinic days, so Maureen had timed things so that she would arrive in Clifden at around ten-thirty, just about the same time as the nurse was starting. She knew that there probably wouldn't be any patients queueing until after eleven, so that would give them a good half-hour to chat.

As the city gave way to the open countryside out past the university on the N59, subtle signs of spring were to be seen on the land. Some trees had put out a few tentative leaves to test the weather before bursting into full foliage, and here and there enthusiastic householders had cut the grass outside their homes, more to encourage new growth than out of necessity.

Beyond Oughterard things were different. Here, in the barren, rocky landscape, winter was continuing to hold on for a little longer. There was little sign of any growth, and of course the wild bog flowers in yellow and purple had not yet put in an appearance.

The never-ending roadworks on the main Clifden road slowed Maureen down with their long stretches of single file traffic controlled by the traditional 'Stop/Go' lollipops. At this hour it didn't seem like there was much actual work going on, but the smell of fresh tar filled the air indicating that somewhere something was happening.

Lyons pulled up outside Tolan's chemist shop at ten thirty-five. She spotted Mary Drinan struggling out of her little Toyota, a few cars ahead of her. Tolan's was at the foot of the hill on Market Street, and with Mary's car facing up the road towards the Atlantic Coast Hotel, extra effort was needed to free herself from the little car.

When Mary was safely anchored on the pavement, Lyons approached her and introduced herself.

"I was hoping we could have a chat about Paddy O'Shaughnessy, Nurse Drinan," Lyons said.

"Oh please, call me Mary, everyone does. Yes, of course. Just let me put my things into the office, and see if there is anyone waiting. I doubt it to be honest, they're usually much later than this, but you never know."

The two women walked back down to Tolan's. The girls in the shop greeted Mary warmly with the usual comments about the weather, and looked curiously at her new-found friend.

Lyons busied herself browsing the display of makeup and nail varnishes on the brightly lit shelving that ran along one side of the compact shop, and soon Mary reappeared carrying just a large handbag.

"There's no one here yet. Will we go and get a cup of tea?" Mary asked.

"Fine. I'm sure you know a quiet place," Lyons said.

Mary Drinan left instructions with the girl in charge of the shop to come and fetch her if anyone showed up for the clinic, saying that they would be in the little blue tea shop just up the street.

When they were settled with a generous pot of tea and a homemade scone apiece in the teashop, Lyons began to quiz the nurse about the victim.

"How long have you been attending Mr O'Shaughnessy, Mary?"

"It's about three years now. He became a patient after he was treated in Galway for a bout of pneumonia that he got in February that year. I remember because it was a very wet winter, and the turf stack that he had at the side of the house had become soaked with rain, so the poor man had almost no fire. And of course, that little cottage of his was so damp. Not fit for sheep if you ask me," she said. "So I started visiting him after that, but to be fair he recovered quite quickly, and there'd not been too much wrong with him since, until, you know…" she said.

"In general terms then, he was in pretty good shape. Any concerns at all about him?" Lyons said.

"Well, you can never be completely relaxed about these old-timers. Once they have had a bout of pneumonia, they are quite susceptible to another one, especially in very harsh winter. So, he would have been grand for the summer months, but once November comes, I'd be keeping a closer eye on him," the nurse said.

"How many more years do you think he might have had?"

"Sad as it seems, these old bachelors don't usually live much beyond eighty. They often don't eat very well, and if they get any infection at all, it often turns serious before anyone knows they are sick. Strangely, the fact that they live alone and don't socialize much helps to keep them away from most things, but I have only one man on my books over eighty, and he's just eighty-one."

"You must have chatted a good bit when you visited Paddy. Can you tell me anything about his past, his family?"

"Paddy was a very private man, Maureen. But we did chat a bit, especially when he wasn't feeling too well."

"Did he have any family that you know of?" Lyons asked.

"He had a brother, Donal, I think his name was. He lived somewhere near Cork, but he died last year. Paddy managed to get to the funeral. He was pretty upset about it, it seems they were close at one stage, but lost touch a bit later on. You know how it is," the nurse said.

"How did he get about around here? He doesn't seem to have had a car."

"He drove the old van up to about two years ago, but no, he used to walk down to the road. People are good with lifts hereabouts. If you stand there for a few minutes, you usually get picked up. There's a lot of local traffic and he was well known. If he needed to go further afield there's a bus from Clifden. When he went to the funeral, he got the bus into Galway, and got trains from there. When he got back, he was complaining that his nephew wouldn't even give him a lift back home. He wasn't happy about that."

"Mary, to be honest we're struggling with this one to find some motive for his killing. We're a bit stuck. It seems a very unlikely case from many angles. Do you happen to know if he had a bank account?"

"Oh yes, he had, and he had a debit card. One time when he was in bed sick he gave it to me with the PIN number to get him some groceries and medication. I know I'm not supposed to do that, I hope I'm not in trouble?"

"No, no, not at all. It's just information about him we are looking for. You're being very helpful." She smiled, and Mary looked reassured.

"What do you know of his past before he came to Derrygimlagh?"

"Not much, to be honest. He was in England for much of his working life, I think, but one time when he was a bit chatty he told me that he and his brother both worked for their uncle years ago. The uncle had a pub in Ballina. He worked there for a few years in the 1960s. He said his uncle was really sound, he was good to them both, and of course the pub trade was a lot better in those days before all this drink driving nonsense started!"

Just then the girl from the chemist's shop came in and told Mary that a client had arrived to see her. Lyons felt that there was not a lot more that Mary could tell her at this point, so she told Mary to go on, and she stayed behind and paid the bill for the teas and scones.

* * *

It was still early when Lyons had finished interviewing the nurse, so she decided to pay a quick call on Sergeant Mulholland to see if she could pick up any little scraps of information from his local knowledge.

Mulholland had his customary cup of tea in front of him at the desk when Lyons entered the station.

"Good morning, Séan. I was in the town and I just thought I'd drop in and see if there was much talk in the pub about Paddy O'Shaughnessy – any theories forming?"

"Ah, Maureen. Come on in and have a cup of tea," Mulholland said.

"Na, you're grand, Sean. But tell me, has there been much talk around the town about the fire and Paddy's death?"

"Oh, you can be sure there's little else being talked about, Maureen. And of course, everyone wants answers. Some of the men living alone out the road are feeling a bit vulnerable, you know, after what happened."

"But have you managed to pick up anything useful from all the chat?"

"Not a bit of it – just lots of gossip. There's been talk about a gang out from the city, but nothing that convinces me. Someone would have seen them, and why would they target poor Paddy in any case. The man had almost nothing to his name."

"No pet theories of your own then?" Lyons said.

"I'll leave the detecting to you, Maureen, and that inspector fella. Murder is a bit above my pay grade, you know."

Realising that there was nothing more to be learned from Sergeant Mulholland, Lyons left, and returned to the city.

# Chapter Ten

When Hays arrived at Mill Street, he went to the lock-up to throw his eye over the BMW. The car wasn't badly damaged at all. One of the rear windows had been smashed, and the back seat was blackened where some burning newspapers had landed, but as the upholstery was leather, it hadn't really burned. That said, the car was a bit of a mess, but not beyond repair.

Hays removed the tax and insurance discs from the windscreen and went inside.

When John O'Connor arrived in the incident room shortly after nine, Hays gave him the two discs from the BMW and asked him to get the details of the car's owner.

"Do you mind if I get Sally to do it, boss? I want to get on with the jigsaw puzzle." O'Connor said.

"No problem, John, just as long as I have the information quickly. Whatever."

Hays then went to his own office and put a call through to Superintendent Plunkett to bring him up to date.

"An eventful couple of days to be sure," Plunkett said. "Are you OK for resources, Mick?"

"Yes, thanks, sir, for now at least. It's quite a complex case though, so we may have to pull in more people."

"That's fine, just let me know what you need. Better not to let it drag out too long for the want of a few extra bodies. It's the start of the tourist season out in Clifden, and they'll be going nuts out there if it's not sorted quickly," Plunkett said. "How's Sergeant Lyons doing?"

"Terrific, sir, we really should try and get her made up to inspector soon, she's well able for it."

"Yes, I heard you two were becoming a formidable team," he said without a hint of irony.

"We work well together. She's great at getting information out of people before they know it," Hays said.

"Yes, well keep up the good work, and let me know if you need anything," Plunkett said.

Superintendent Plunkett was a good man to work for. Oh sure, he could be full of bullshit when the occasion demanded it, but he was almost always supportive, even when someone cocked up. He was well connected too: a member of the Galway Lions Club, and various other organizations that allowed him to mix with the great and the good of the city.

The next phone call Hays made was to the forensic lab. He was lucky to get Sinéad on the phone, and he explained about the car, asking to have it collected and brought to their garage.

"I'd really appreciate it if you could fast track it for me, Sinéad. I don't want the trail to go cold."

"No problem, sir, after all it's not often that a man gives a girl a present of a BMW, even if it is somewhat fire damaged! I'll get two of the boys onto it straight away. Should have preliminaries for you by this evening."

"Great, thanks. I owe you one."

"No, sir, you owe me many more than that," she said, laughing, and hung up.

Sally Fahy knocked on the door of Hays' office. She had a slip of paper in her hand.

"Yes, Sally, come in. What's up?"

"It's the car details, sir. I have them here. It's owned by a Mr Rory O'Keeffe from Limerick. He reported it stolen from outside his house earlier in the week."

"Well, could you get onto Limerick and tell them we have it. Talk to Detective Aidan Phelan if you can get him, he knows me. Ask them if they could stay off it and let us handle it, as it may be connected to another enquiry here. Oh, and see if you can get a phone number for Rory O'Keeffe, his insurance company probably have his mobile number on file," Hays said. He then noticed that Sally looked distinctly uneasy.

"What's up, Sally?"

"Nothing, sir, it's just that a lot of this is police work. Are you sure it's OK for me to be doing it? I'd hate anyone to get into trouble," she said.

"Sit down for a minute, Sally, let's have a wee chat, shall we?"

Sally sat down not quite sure what was coming.

"Sally, I don't know if you realize this, but you're better at police work, as you call it, than half the people at this station, except of course for my team that I have selected very carefully over a few years now."

Sally blushed and wriggled a little in her chair, not knowing how to respond.

"If you wanted to become a detective Garda, you'd make a good one. But don't say anything now, just think it over."

"Thanks, sir," she said, getting up from the chair and feeling about two feet taller. As she left the room she turned at the door and said to Hays, "Thank you very much, sir, it means a lot."

Hays studied the piece of paper that Sally had left on his desk. It had O'Keeffe's address on it, as well as his occupation and a few other relevant details about his driving license, and the fact that his wife was also a named driver on the policy. He lifted the phone and dialled the number on the page. It answered promptly.

"Rory O'Keeffe," said the voice at the other end of the line.

"Good morning, Mr O'Keeffe. This is Detective Inspector Michael Hays from Galway. I'm calling about a car." He read out the registration number from the page in front of him.

"Great, you've found it! Where is it?" O'Keeffe asked.

"Firstly, sir, can you confirm that you are the registered owner of that vehicle, and that you reported it stolen earlier in the week?" Hays asked.

"Yes, yes. But have you found it? Is it OK? I know it's only an 07 but I really love that car," O'Keeffe replied.

"Well, yes, sir, we have found it. But it's not all good news I'm afraid. Firstly, it may have been involved in a crime, so we need to keep it here for a while. It may be evidence," Hays told the man.

"I see. That's not good. What type of crime?"

"I'm sorry, Mr O'Keeffe, I'm not able to discuss that aspect of things just yet. But there's more. An attempt was made to burn the car out. Now fortunately a fire appliance was driving past at the time and put it out quite quickly, but there is some damage."

"Oh shit. Sorry. Yes, I see. So, it sounds like I'll have to claim on the insurance then."

"Probably best. We'll give you a crime report in respect of the theft, and if we can help in any other way, let me know. Was there anything in the car that you need?" Hays asked.

"Nothing much. A few CDs and a small jar of parking coins, but I'm not bothered about any of those. It's the car I'll miss. And the insurance will give me bugger all for it. Sorry. I really liked it."

"Yes, well I'm sorry for your loss, Mr O'Keeffe. If it's any help, I can send the tax disc back to you. There's almost ten months unexpired on it, so you'll get quite a bit back."

"Yes, thanks, that will help a bit. The tax is quite high. How did they take it? BMWs are supposed to be burglar proof."

"These scallywags do this all the time. If they want it, they take it. Nothing is burglar proof. OK, I'll get my sergeant to send on the tax and insurance discs. Just one more thing, Mr O'Keeffe, where were you the night before last?"

"Aw, c'mon. You can't be serious?" O'Keeffe protested.

"Just routine, Mr O'Keeffe, just routine."

"As it happens, I was at a work do. I had to get a lift of course, but I was out till about half-past one, then got a taxi home. It was on the company's account, so there will be a record."

Hays thanked the man and said they might have to be back in touch at some stage, but that he shouldn't worry. He might just be asked to make a statement.

# Chapter Eleven

Garda John O'Connor and Sally Fahy were working with the little bag of paper scraps that had been found in the burnt-out shell of Paddy O'Shaughnessy's cottage. There were about twenty-five pieces in all, not any one of which was big enough to make sense. One fragment was definitely a bank statement, just as Sinéad had said, but the account number was missing, and just the first two digits of the branch sort code could be deciphered.

"It's nine seven," said Sally, "that means it's a National Bank account," she said.

"How the hell do you know that?" O'Connor asked.

"It's easy. Nine seven is National, nine three is AIB, nine zero is Bank of Ireland, and so on."

"But what actual branch?"

"That's the tricky bit. Logically, it should be Clifden, but that's already been checked out, and his account isn't there. Maybe we could get on to National Bank's HQ and ask them?"

"Not likely. How many Paddy O'Shaughnessy's, P. O'Shaughnessy, Peadar O'Shaughnessy etc. do you think they have? They'd just laugh at us."

"OK then, let's keep going, see what else we can find," Sally said, a little disappointed with the rebuke.

"You keep going, I'm off to lunch. See you later," he said, getting up and putting on his uniform jacket. "Want anything brought back?"

"No thanks, you're OK. I'll take a break myself in a while."

Sally was determined to find something useful before he got back. She had been made to look silly with her suggestion about calling the bank's head office, and it didn't sit well with her.

Some of the paper fragments had handwriting on them, and some of that was pretty shaky, as you would expect from an old person. Some of it was even in pencil. As she fiddled with the tiny scraps of paper, trying to line up the torn edges, suddenly she saw it. It wasn't all on one piece, but in the same shaky hand, numbers. Numbers that made up the six-digit sort code of a bank branch. Nine seven, six one, zero six.

Sally went to the nearest PC and called up a sort code look up programme. When she put the numbers in, the programme promptly returned "National Bank, Westport."

"Bingo," she said to herself, "gotcha!"

Sally was tempted to go straight to Hays who was still in his office with the news, but then on reflection, she decided not to do that. It would be better, she felt, to let John O'Connor take the credit for the discovery, and if he decided to mention her efforts to the boss, all to the good. After all, she wasn't a detective – yet.

* * *

When O'Connor returned from a short lunch break, Sally shared the news with him.

"Amazing, Sal, how do you do it? But are we sure that's what those numbers are? It could be part of a phone number or something," he said.

"Well, let's check. Call the bank and see if they can confirm that he has an account there," Sally said.

O'Connor looked up the Westport branch of the National Bank on a PC and placed the call. When he told the girl of his enquiry, she put him through to the manager, who was disinclined to impart any information about one of his customers. After some persuasion he eventually confirmed that they had a customer by that name with an address in County Galway, but he would give no further details of any kind.

O'Connor knocked on Hays' door.

"Come in, John. What's up?" Hays said.

"We found O'Shaughnessy's bank account, sir, or, to be accurate, Sally found it. The bank has confirmed the existence of the account, but won't give out any further information on the basis of the Data Protection Act," O'Connor said.

"Data Protection Act my arse! But well done you two, that's great. Did you get the name of the person that you spoke to?"

"Yes, boss. It's a Mr Neville Watson. He seemed to want to help, but he was very guarded."

"We'll see about that. Did you tell him O'Shaughnessy is dead?"

"No, sir. I wasn't going to give anything away as he was being so awkward. Should I have?"

"No, you did right. That's great work, John, and Sally too. Well done."

Sally continued to work on the remaining bits of burnt paper that had been recovered from the house. She had a feeling that they had more to tell, and after another hour working with tweezers and sticky tape, her efforts were rewarded. She found some other fragments that she was able to put together that seemed to come from a flyer or small pamphlet. It had been issued by one Jerome Kelly, who described himself as a QFA, which Sally knew to be a qualified financial advisor. Sally was curious to know why Paddy O'Shaughnessy would have such an item in amongst his meagre belongings, but she wasted no time in reporting it to her boss.

"Hmm," mused Hays when she brought the information to him. "It's probably nothing, but we need to follow it up just the same. Is there a phone number on the leaflet?" he asked.

"Yes, but it's incomplete, and it's a mobile. There doesn't seem to be a landline number, unless it was burnt in the fire," Sally replied.

"OK, Sally, well dig around a bit more and see if you can find anything on this Jerome Kelly fella, and let us know."

# Chapter Twelve

The entire team were back in the incident room by four that afternoon. After a quick introduction, Hays asked them one by one to give details of what they had learned during the day.

Lyons started with all the information she had extracted from Mary Drinan that morning. The team were impressed with the amount of detail that Lyons had collected, and Hays said that they could now start to build a picture of the victim.

O'Connor told the team about the bank details that Sally had unearthed. She had been right to give it to O'Connor, and not directly to Hays, as John was now singing her praises instead of thinking she was out to better him. "Good call," she thought to herself.

Finally, Eamon Flynn, who had spent much of the day over with the forensic team working on the car, shared his story.

"The car thieves had clearly meant the BMW to burn out completely, destroying any evidence that they may have left behind in it, but as we know, that was not to be," Flynn reported.

"The good news is that there are quite a few clear fingerprint images in the car, and even some potential DNA from a half-eaten sandwich in the passenger's footwell. Forensics are lifting the prints now, and should be able to try and match them overnight."

Just as the briefing was coming to an end, Sally Fahy piped up. "There's just one other thing," she said, hesitating a little.

"Yes, Sally, what is it?"

"Well it's just that other piece of paper that was found, you know the Jerome Kelly thing."

"Oh yes, anything on that?" Hays asked, a little impatiently.

"Well I managed to figure out the rest of the phone number, and I looked up the register of QFAs that the Central Bank keeps online. Kelly was a QFA up to about five years ago, and then he was de-listed. There's no information on why, but he's no longer a QFA."

"Well maybe that leaflet is older than five years. You know how these old codgers like to hang on to everything."

"No, sir, that's not it. You see the mobile number on the leaflet is a Tesco Mobile number, and they have only been in Ireland for three years, so it has to be more recent than that."

"Did you get a chance to see if we have anything on file for Jerome Kelly QFA? Anything on Pulse, or whatever?" Lyons asked.

"No, boss, not yet. But I'll have a look before I go tonight. And I'll contact the Central Bank and see what they can tell me too," Sally said.

"OK, good work. Let us know what you find," Hays said.

"That's great progress, thanks· everyone. OK. Tasks for tomorrow then. Someone needs to go to Westport and give that stuffy bank manager a good shake up. I want O'Shaughnessy's bank statements for the last two years, and any other details that we can dig up. Who's up for that?" Hays asked.

They all looked from one to another, but no one volunteered.

"Very well, that'll be you then, Maureen. I know you love the wild west so much," Hays said.

"Thanks a bunch, boss," she said.

"Next, we need someone to work on whoever stole the BMW. I'm expecting the fingerprints will match some well-known scrotes, so, Eamon, can you follow up on that when the information comes through?

"John, you and Sally, our new 'A' team, can you dig into O'Shaughnessy's brother? Look up RIP.IE and see what you can find out about family connections, that sort of thing. That's it for now folks. We'll have another briefing at one o'clock tomorrow. Maureen, if you're not back by then, can you call in? Thanks."

* * *

Hays didn't go home straight away, and he noticed Maureen hanging around for a while too. He called her into his office.

"Sorry about the job in Westport, but to be honest, you're the best person for it. You have a way of getting people to talk that no one else on the team can match."

"Now you're trying to butter me up," she said.

"No, I'm not. You know me better than that. In fact, I was just saying the same thing to Superintendent Plunkett earlier."

"Oh, so you were discussing me then. I thought my ears were burning."

"We were saying that you would make a great detective inspector."

"I don't know if I'm ready for that yet, Mick. Do you really think I am?" she asked.

"Yes, I do. I've been really impressed with your work, and your ability to delegate and manage the younger, less experienced members of the team. Talking of which, what do you think of Sally Fahy?"

"She's a topper. Would make a good detective. That Tesco Mobile thing wouldn't have occurred to most people. Why?"

"I was thinking exactly the same. Why don't you have a word with her, you know, woman to woman, as it were?"

Maureen's eyes flared.

"Oh, and about Westport," Hays added, "would you like me to come out with you? You can lead, it's just for the company."

"Tell you what. Why don't we go and get a bite to eat? We can talk about this inspector thing, and maybe you should come to Westport with me," she said.

"There's just one thing ... it's a very early start," she said with a smile.

# Chapter Thirteen

They set off for Westport at eight o'clock the following morning. Hays had stayed over, and before they left Maureen had made them both a good plate of scrambled eggs and bacon and some strong hot coffee.

They talked more about Maureen becoming an inspector on the journey. Hays told her that she would have a lot of support from within the ranks, which was even more important than the exams. Maureen expressed concern about how they would handle it at a personal level, and they agreed that the rank didn't really make a difference, in fact, if anything, it would be easier if they were of equal rank.

Lyons leaned over and kissed him on the cheek.

"You're a good man, Mick Hays."

They travelled on in silence, but both could feel that the bond between them had grown a little closer. It was a good feeling.

They arrived in Westport at nine forty-five and easily found the National Bank branch and parked outside. To fill the fifteen minutes before the bank opened, they went for coffee in a nearby café.

By ten o'clock there was a small queue outside the bank. They joined the back of it and filed in along with the other customers. Once inside, they asked the nearest floorwalker if they could see the manager, Mr Watson.

"Do you have an appointment, sir?" she asked politely.

Hays didn't reply but reached into his pocket and produced his warrant card, holding it up so that the girl could see it clearly.

"Right. I'll see if he is available. Just wait there a moment, please."

When the girl returned she ushered the two detectives into a small gloomy office at the rear of the building. The room was painted in the wrong colour of sickly yellow, and there was just one small barred window high in the wall behind where Neville Watson sat at a desk straight out of the 1970s. The only other furniture in the dingy office were two chairs, upholstered in black vinyl, facing the desk, and a set of bookshelves packed with large plastic-bound training manuals that were too big for the shelves, so that they looked as if they might fall to the floor at any moment. Lyons noticed that the grey carpet in front of the visitors' chairs was worn through, and the paler sisal backing was showing.

"Good morning, officers, how can I help you?" Watson said, standing up and extending his hand to Hays. Hays said nothing, allowing Lyons to do the talking as he had promised he would. Lyons introduced them, and when they were all seated, continued, "Mr Watson, can you confirm for us that you hold an account here for a Mr

Paddy, or Patrick O'Shaughnessy with an address at Derrygimlagh, County Galway?"

Hays was relieved that Lyons was leading. He had taken an instant dislike to the bank manager, which was unusual for him, so he was pleased to be able to remain silent.

"Let me see," said Watson, turning to the computer screen on his desk and tapping a few keys with two fingers. After a couple of moments of silence, he said to no one in particular, "The system is very slow today for some reason." Moments turned to minutes, but at last he said, "Ah yes, we do appear to have an account in that name. Patrick O'Shaughnessy, yes I think that's the one."

"Mr Watson," Lyons went on in a rather brusque tone. "May I ask you to positively confirm the fact? It's important to our enquiries."

"Yes, I can confirm," he said.

"Thank you. May I ask what the current balance in Mr O'Shaughnessy's account is?"

"Oh, I couldn't possibly divulge that kind of information. I'm afraid we have very strict rules about customer confidentiality you know," Watson said rather smugly.

While Lyons and Watson were locked in some kind of verbal duel, Hays had quietly repositioned his chair, and he could just about make out the figures on Watson's screen. Lyons decided to take another tack.

"Very well. Could you tell me if there is a debit card connected to that account please?" she asked.

"Yes, yes, there is, issued last year and still in date."

"Thank you. Now can you say when the card was last used to make an ATM withdrawal?" she persisted.

"I'm sorry, Sergeant, the Data Protection Act does not permit me to divulge any information pertinent to the data subject's financial affairs," Watson said.

"Mr Watson, the Data Protection Act does not apply in the case of the deceased. All protection for a data subject expires at the moment of death, and I can assure you, Paddy O'Shaughnessy is most assuredly deceased."

"Oh, my goodness. I didn't know. When did he pass?"

"A few days ago, and we believe he was assisted in his passing, so we are conducting a murder investigation, and we would appreciate the cooperation of the bank."

"Oh my gosh, well of course we must freeze the account immediately. We have to do that as soon as a death is notified to us, pending the issue of probate. May I ask how he died?"

"You can ask, but I'm not going to tell you," said Lyons. "Now if I could just have the information that I asked for, please," she said.

"Look, I'm not at all comfortable about this. I'll have to consult head office before I can release any information. Could you come back tomorrow perhaps?" Watson asked.

Lyons remained silent for a moment. Hays recognized the signs and almost felt sorry for the man.

"Mr Watson, you have no legitimate reason not to supply the information that I have requested. Now if you insist on being obstructive, we will indeed return tomorrow. At that time, we will be accompanied by inspectors from both the Revenue Commissioners and the Central Bank of Ireland, and if they find one, just one, account belonging to a resident that is being held at this branch as a non-resident account for the purpose of avoiding tax, I will personally see that you are prosecuted for aiding and abetting a citizen, or citizens, to defraud the State, and if convicted, that charge carries a jail sentence."

Watson started to protest, but before he could speak, Lyons went on, "You are already guilty of obstructing the Gardaí in the execution of their duty. True, a lesser crime, but a crime nonetheless. So, will you please stop pissing about before I get really angry!"

Magnificent, Hays thought. The colour had drained completely from Watson's face. He took a moment to compose himself and then went on, "O'Shaughnessy has, or should I say 'had', €18,274.12 in his account. The ATM card was last used about three weeks ago to withdraw sixty euro."

"And where did that withdrawal take place, Mr Watson?"

"I'll have to check the reference number on the transaction," he said turning back to the computer and navigating with the mouse before typing a few more characters with his two rather shaky index fingers.

"It appears to have been used in Clifden, at the AIB branch," he said in a very subdued manner.

"Appears?" Lyons went back at him.

"No, it was used at the AIB branch in Clifden. I think it's down at the bottom of the town near the junction with the Westport road," he added, trying to get back on some sort of normal terms with Lyons.

"Thank you. Now before we leave, I'll need copies of the statements from that account going back two years, and can you tell us if O'Shaughnessy had any other accounts here?"

Watson turned back to the computer to see if he could coax the requested information from it.

"It appears not," he said after a short interval.

"Appears?" Lyons said.

"There are no other accounts," he said. He lifted the phone and spoke to a girl called Gráinne and asked her to prepare the statements that the detective had requested.

An icy silence pervaded the manager's office.

"Is that all?" he said nervously.

"That will do, for now, Mr Watson," Lyons said.

"Then perhaps you could wait outside for the statements. Gráinne will have them ready for you in a few minutes."

Hays and Lyons got up and left the room without another word.

Outside, in the public area, they waited for almost ten minutes before a chubby, short, dark haired girl with glasses approached them carrying a large white envelope.

"People usually print these at home, you know. We don't really have facilities here for batch printing statements," she said, clearly not happy with the break in the bank's procedures that were designed to ensure maximum inconvenience and cost for its customers, and minimum cost and workload for the bank.

Lyons thought about it for a second and Hays braced himself for round two, but she just glared at the girl and took the envelope without a word.

Outside the bank, walking to the car Hays asked Lyons, "What raw meat did you have for breakfast then?"

"Sanctimonious prick. And did you see the state of his office? Our cells are in better condition."

"Remind me never to cross you early in the morning," he said.

"Oh, I can be just as vicious in the afternoon, I promise you," she said.

"And what was all that bullshit about the DPA? Is that true?"

"Sort of. The DPA doesn't actually refer to deceased subjects, so it can easily be argued that they are excluded by omission. The Freedom of Information Act is different. It restricts personal details to executors and next of kin."

"So, who's been swatting for their Inspector's exam then?"

"I'm just looking at it to see what's involved, that's all," she replied.

\* \* \*

They set off back along the N84 to Galway taking them through Partry, Ballinrobe and on into Headford before the late morning traffic slowed them down as they approached the city.

"Why are you so set on this inspector thing, boss?" she asked.

"I don't know if you're fully in the picture, Maureen. Things are going to change a lot for the Gardaí in Galway over the next few years. The force will be expanded, and more responsibility will be devolved to an extended regional crime squad when we get the new headquarters," Hays explained.

"I want to build a really strong team. I want us to be the 'A' team – the 'go to' team for serious crime. We're doing pretty well so far. You're a very good detective, and ballsy too. Flynn is coming along nicely. He's a terrier. Never lets go of a situation till he's got to the bottom of it.

That's very useful. O'Connor is a good lad too. He's great with data and all that tech. That's going to become more and more important as time goes by. And then there's Sally. If we could get her into the team, even as a detective Garda it would be terrific."

"But that leaves you short of a sergeant."

"No, if you move up, Flynn gets that slot."

"And what about you, boss?" she asked.

"Here's where it gets clever. Plunkett has told me, off the record of course, that they are going to create a new unofficial rank of senior detective inspector. It's not 'Chief' like they have in the UK, but there will be a pay scale for it. The new unofficial rank will assume full operational duties for crime, leaving the superintendent to focus on PR and administration."

"I see. I'd better get my books out. Oh, and I'll have another word with Sally – but don't go getting any ideas just because she's blonde now, do you hear?" she said, hitting his leg.

# Chapter Fourteen

When they got back to Mill Street Station, the team had gone to lunch, all except for Sally Fahy who was still sitting at her desk.

Lyons gave her the envelope of bank statements and asked her to key them into a spreadsheet so that the transactions could be grouped and analysed.

"When John gets back from lunch, ask him to examine the details and do me a one-pager with the transactions sorted into ATM, bank transfers, lodgements and so on, by time, so we can see what's going on," Lyons said.

Sally agreed, and opened up Microsoft Excel on her PC.

"Oh, and while you were out, this came in from forensics for Inspector Hays," she said, handing Lyons a sealed brown envelope.

"Anything more on our mysterious QFA, Mr Kelly?" Lyon asked.

"Yes, there is. Turns out he was de-listed for 'conduct unbecoming of a professional financial advisor'. Roughly translated, it means he was conning old folks out of their savings."

"Interesting. So, what's he doing in these parts pretending to be a QFA then I wonder? Anything on Pulse?"

"No, not a thing. But I'm not finished yet. I'll talk to the consumer complaints people, see if they have anything. And I've been on to Tesco. They're trying to get an address for him, or perhaps his bank details so we can find out a bit more about him," Sally said.

"Great. Let us know when you have anything."

\* \* \*

Lyons went into Hays' office and handed the envelope to him.

"Good. It'll be the information from the car. Let's see what they found," he said opening the envelope and taking out two sheets of densely printed paper.

"Ah, nice one, Sinéad," he said as he read the information, "she's managed to lift some excellent prints from the inside of the door handle, and the base of the gear stick."

Handing the sheets to Lyons, Hays said, "Get these run through Print-Track will you, and see if we can identify them?"

Print-Track was a relatively new service that held a database of finger and palm prints of known offenders. It had recently been rolled out to all Garda Stations, so now prints could be scanned in and compared to thousands of samples held on file very quickly. In Dublin and Cork they even had it hooked up to mobile devices so that matches could be made if a suspect vehicle was stopped. It was planned ultimately to integrate the system with Interpol and Europol as well as the Police Service of Northern Ireland.

* * *

Lyons was back in twenty minutes with a big grin on her face.

"The clowns must have thought that the car would burn out completely. We're looking at two low-lifes from Limerick. Two brothers, Jazz and Dingo Morrissey if you don't mind."

"Fabulous! Is Eamon back from lunch?" Hays asked.

"Yes, he's at his desk. Will I ask him to come in?"

"Yes, please."

Flynn joined Hays and Lyons in Hays' office.

"What's up, boss?" he asked.

"Eamon, the very man. We need to interview two charmers from Limerick. Jazz and Dingo Morrissey by name, and they'll be well known to the Gardaí in Limerick I imagine. Can you get on to Henry Street? Ask for Inspector Pat Dineen, I know him pretty well. Get him to lift the two boys and bring them in. You can tell Pat what it's all about but ask him to keep the master criminals in the dark till you get there. When he tells you he has them, can you go down and frighten the shite out of them? Pat will give you another detective to help you out."

"OK, boss. Do you think they murdered the old guy?" Flynn asked.

"No, but I think there's a good chance they torched the house. I want to know why, and more particularly, who put them up to it. From their sheet it looks like they're probably small time, and quite stupid too. If you tell them that they're implicated in a murder, they'll probably sing like a couple of canaries."

When Eamon Flynn had left the office, John O'Connor knocked and came in.

"We've done a quick analysis of O'Shaughnessy's bank account. Here's a breakdown," O'Connor said, handing Hays a sheet of paper.

"We've broken it down as best we can. It looks as if he was receiving two pensions. One from here at the usual non-contributory rate. You can see that going in every Friday in euro. Then there's a pension from the UK in sterling. That goes in every four weeks. It's a lot less, but worth having all the same. It's about sixty euro a week, presumably because he didn't work there all his life," O'Connor reported.

"Then there's the outgoings. Simple enough. Electricity, property tax, both paid by direct debit monthly, and his cash withdrawals of about a hundred euro a week on average. He paid the chemist too, normally around a hundred a month. It's no wonder he had accumulated quite a bit."

O'Connor went on, "Oh, and Sally found something else too. Every three months there's a US dollar credit to the account. The amount varies a bit, but it's usually around three hundred dollars. There's a reference number, but I can't make any sense of it. Sally is looking into it now to see if she can find out what it's all about."

"Great. That's good work. Thanks, John. Let us know if you can trace the American payments."

When John O'Connor had left the room, Lyons asked Hays if she thought that Flynn could handle the Limerick interviews on his own.

"I'm sure he can. Anyway, Pat will keep an eye on him. He needs this if he's to develop his skills, and anyway I doubt if our two heroes are exactly the Kray twins."

"Oh, and Sally found out a bit more about the elusive Mr Jerome Kelly." Lyons went on to relate the information that had been gleaned by the young civilian.

"Wow. OK, let her at it a bit longer, then I think we need to have a word with the ex-QFA, don't you?"

"Definitely," she said.

# Chapter Fifteen

Eamon Flynn drove the journey to Limerick in just over an hour and a half. He arrived at Henry Street Station before six and asked to see Inspector Pat Dineen.

After a short wait, a tall thin man in his late forties or early fifties entered the public area of the station where Flynn was sat waiting. The man wore a well-fitting navy suit with a pale blue shirt and a two-tone blue striped tie. His shoes were highly polished, and his neatly trimmed grey hair completed the picture of someone who not only cares about his appearance but minds himself well in an overall sense.

He made straight for Flynn with his hand extended and a welcoming smile on his face.

"Detective Flynn, I'm Pat Dineen. Welcome to Limerick," he said.

"Good afternoon, Inspector," Flynn said, shaking the other's hand, and noting that Pat Dineen had a firm and confident grip.

"You must be hungry after your drive. Why don't we go around to the Glentworth and get a bite to eat? Our two clients won't miss us for half an hour, and I can bring you up to speed. And by the way, it's Pat – we don't stand on ceremony here," the inspector said.

"Oh, right. Thanks. Yes, I'm famished actually, and I'm Eamon."

Dineen told the desk sergeant where they were off to and said they would be back before seven, and if anything arose, he could be contacted by phone.

"The Glentworth isn't great, but they're used to us dropping in at all hours, and they'll be able to fix us up with something tasty."

The two men headed out of the station and walked across the road up Glentworth Street to the hotel.

"So, how long have you been working with Mick?" Dineen asked.

"Nearly four years now. Ever since I started wearing my own clothes." This was how detectives normally described their transition from uniformed Garda to detective.

"You'll know him well. I've known him since Templemore. We trained together. He's one of the good guys. You're lucky," Dineen said.

"Yes, he's very good to work with. Tell me, was he ever married? None of us can find out."

"No, never married. He had a long-term girlfriend for about ten years up to three years ago or so, but for some reason they never tied the knot. I think she finally got fed up with the crazy hours and moved on."

At the Glentworth the two settled into easy chairs in the lounge with a low brown coffee table between them.

Almost at once a waitress with dyed blonde hair and a chubby, happy face appeared carrying a metal tray.

"Good evening, Mr Dineen," she said, "what can I get you then?"

"It could be a long night, Sheila. How about two of your best mixed grills with loads of brown bread and a big pot of tea?" And, turning to Flynn, he said, "Would that be OK with you, Eamon?"

"Terrific, thanks," he replied, not at all used to this kind of hospitality.

"So, what's the crack with these two clowns then, Eamon?" Dineen asked.

Flynn went on to explain the reason for their interest in the two Limerick thugs, and that his main concern at this stage was to establish who had set them up to burn down Paddy O'Shaughnessy's house, and why.

"Inspector Hays said you might be able to give me a detective to help with the interview. Someone who knows these guys and their form."

"You're looking at him," Dineen said. "I've met these two lads a few times now and charged them more than once. I know their form, and how to get them to talk. They think they're clever, but they're not. They think because they know the procedure they can outwit us, or bamboozle us with 'no comment', but so far, it's Morrisseys nil, Gardaí three. They have both been inside a few times for burglary, car theft and robbery with intent. I'll be your wingman on this one."

"That's great, Pat, much appreciated," Flynn said.

"But you lead the questioning. I'll just sit there looking menacing to remind them how it went down the last few times."

The two men finished their substantial meal. Dineen paid for both of them ignoring Flynn's protestations, and they returned to the station feeling well satisfied and ready to tackle the Morrissey brothers.

* * *

The Morrisseys' solicitor, one Eric Tyndall, had arrived some time ago, and had consulted with the two boys to see if they could cook up some kind of make-shift story to keep the Gardaí happy. Tyndall was waiting in reception when Dineen and Flynn walked in. He was a slight man who went only about two-thirds of the way to filling his well-worn grey suit. He was about five foot seven in height, with balding dark hair and thick lensed glasses. Dineen had met him on at least one previous occasion, and if things ran true to form, the solicitor would be of little use to the two suspects.

In the interests of saving time, Dineen had decided to interview the two at the same time, as it was inevitable that they would have synchronized their stories in any case. The two suspects, their solicitor, and Dineen and Flynn, were all packed into the small, drab interview room. The Morrisseys sat facing the door, side by side, with Tyndall at the end of the table, leaving the two detectives with their backs to the door.

Flynn introduced himself and addressing the two, said, "Have you two any idea why you have been brought here?"

"No. Police harassment I suppose. We haven't done anything," the older of the two brothers responded.

"I don't think that's very accurate now, lads, is it?"

"Can you tell us where you were on Wednesday night of this week?" Flynn asked.

"At home, or maybe in the pub. We can't remember," the elder brother continued.

"That's funny. You think you would remember stealing a car and driving to the wilds of Connemara in the middle of the night," Flynn said.

"What's this guy on?" Dingo said, laughing. "Jazz told you, we were at home."

"Then perhaps you can explain how we found your fingerprints and DNA all over a stolen BMW in Galway on Thursday evening?"

"Must be some mistake. Nothing to do with us," the elder brother piped up.

"So, you'll have witnesses then that are prepared to swear you were at home on Wednesday and Thursday?"

"Sure, how many do you want?" Jazz responded, smirking.

"You see, you guys were unlucky. When you thought you had burned out the car, destroying your prints and other evidence, what do you think happened but a fire engine came along and put the fire out before it had really started," Flynn paused, and the brothers looked at each other.

"So, there's no point in denying it, the evidence is clear. You took the car and drove to Galway." Flynn paused to allow the information to sink in.

"But what I really want to know is why you drove all the way out to Derrygimlagh and set the house on fire?" Flynn said, putting down a photograph of O'Shaughnessy's burnt out cottage on the table.

"Nice job. Almost total destruction – but not quite," he said, leaving the innuendo hanging.

"What the fuck are you talking about? Derry what's it... where the fuck is that?"

"It's where you poured petrol in the back door of Paddy O'Shaughnessy's cottage and set it on fire."

Tyndall cleared his throat, and said in a very uncertain voice, "I presume you have some evidence of this accusation, Detective?"

"I'm glad you asked that, Mr Tyndall. Yes, indeed we do. Let's assume that your two clients here did take the BMW and were using it on Wednesday night. We can place the car at the scene quite easily. There are distinctive tyre tracks that belong to the car at the cottage."

"That don't mean shit," said Jazz. "You're just fishing. Don't say no more, Dingo. They can fuck off!"

"Very well then, gents, if that's your attitude, but I should warn you both that we'll probably be charging both of you with murder, or at least accessory after the fact. Now, I need a break. Shall we say thirty minutes?" Flynn and Dineen got up and left the room.

Outside the room, the two detectives walked back to Dineen's office.

"Well done, Eamon. That was a nice touch. When we go back in they'll admit to the car theft. They'll not want to be anywhere near a murder charge, wait till you see."

The half hour flew in quickly with Flynn and Dineen just making small talk about life in the force, and the challenges the Gardaí face with criminals becoming more sophisticated, and, it seemed, more vicious every day.

On the way back to the interview room Flynn said, "How do you think we should play it this time?"

"Just as you were. Get them to confess to the car theft. Then lead them into setting the fire at the house.

Talk about O'Shaughnessy's death, and then they'll probably cough up what they know."

As soon as they were seated back in the interview room, Tyndall spoke up.

"Let's just assume for the moment, hypothetically of course, that my clients did confess to taking the BMW and attempting to set it on fire in Galway, and let's just assume, again hypothetically, that they could be of some help with the, eh… other business, what are we looking at?"

"That's a lot of hypotheses, Mr Tyndall. Here's how I see it. Your two received some instruction somehow to go to Connemara and torch Paddy O'Shaughnessy's house. They went out and pinched a set of wheels, drove to the house and set fire to it. Then they drove to Galway and tried to burn out the car, but that didn't work, as we know, and they left fingerprints and DNA all over it. We might be able to do something about the car theft. It was well insured after all. Not so sure about the arson at the house, that's trickier. But if we had solid information about who was behind it, well, we might possibly be able to do something," Flynn said.

"And what about this accessory stuff," Tyndall went on, thinking he was on a roll.

"Let's see what your clients can tell us about who told them to do this, and why. Then we'll look at the whole picture. So, lads, what can you tell us?" Flynn said.

The boys looked at each other and shrugged.

"OK then," the elder one said.

"We were in the pub Wednesday night and a guy we kinda know came over and gave me a bit of paper with a phone number on it. He said to call it, that there was a handy little job to be done," Jazz said, a bit nervously. "So,

I phoned the number, and this guy told me he wanted a house burnt out in the west. He said there was five hundred euro in it, but it had to be done that night. I asked him how we could be sure that he would pay up, and he said to ask the guy who gave us the number."

Jazz went on to explain that the mysterious bloke on the other end of the phone had texted the coordinates of the location to him, and told him to be careful, that the house could be under watch. Then they went out and got the car. They set off for the house, picking up a can of petrol on the way, and arrived at about three o'clock.

"Well, I should tell you that earlier that same day an old man was found murdered in that house. His body had just been removed a few hours before you got there, so your fire destroyed any forensic evidence that there was," Flynn said.

"Shit. We didn't know that. We thought it was an insurance job. The place looked fucking abandoned to us."

"Well, it wasn't. That was a man's home till you two burnt it out."

"We didn't know, honest," the younger one said.

"Have you still got the guy's number?" Flynn asked.

"Yeah. It'll be in my phone from when he texted me the coordinates," Jazz said, reaching into his pocket and taking out the very latest iPhone. He handed the phone to Flynn. Flynn scrolled down through the text messages until he came to the one that Jazz was talking about and made a note of the number.

"So, what happens now?" Dingo asked.

"Well, we're just about finished here. You'll be kept in for the night, then tomorrow you can both make statements, and we'll see what happens after that. It's not up to me if you're charged or not, that's Inspector Dineen's decision," Flynn said.

Tyndall then addressed the inspector, "I think you'll agree, Inspector, that my clients have been more than helpful with your enquiries. I really think you should consider letting them go, don't you?"

"No, I don't," Dineen replied. "I'll see about it in the morning. It's nearly eleven o'clock. Time for bed, I think."

Dineen got up, followed by Flynn and Tyndall, leaving the two brothers to contemplate their fate.

At the front desk, Dineen told the sergeant to bed the two brothers down for the night, said goodnight to the solicitor, and headed off to his office with Flynn in tow.

"Well, what do you reckon?" Dineen asked when they were seated in his office.

"I hate to say it, but they could easily be telling the truth. What do you think the chances are?" Flynn said.

"You could be right. They tend to do that when they're scared. They're not such hard men really. Anyway, where are you staying tonight?" Dineen asked.

"Oh, I'm not. I'll head back. The boss will want this as soon as possible in the morning, and besides, there will be no traffic on the road at this hour."

"Well, if you're sure. Mind the road though, there are roadworks north of Gort."

"I'll be fine, and thanks for your help, and the meal," Flynn said.

"Don't mention it. You can return the favour if I'm ever up in Galway."

* * *

Flynn set off on the road back to Galway. It was a dreadful night. The rain lashed down on his car and the strong westerly winds buffeted it as he headed north. Fortunately, he was not the type to fall asleep at the wheel, which would have been fatal in those conditions. By the time he reached Gort, about two thirds of the way home, things had improved considerably. The wind was still strong, but the rain had given way to a patchy sky, and from time to time a large full moon broke through, bathing the landscape with an eerie blue light.

Flynn reached home at just after two and was fast asleep ten minutes later.

# Chapter Sixteen

Despite the late hour the previous night, Flynn arrived at the Garda station just before nine the following day. Hays, Lyons and O'Connor were already assembled in the incident room. When Flynn arrived, Hays called the meeting to order.

"OK everyone, we have a lot more information now, so I'd like to go around the room to see what everyone has. John, can we start with you?"

John collected up some papers from his desk and started to address the others.

"Right. Well firstly there's the bank statements. It's all fairly straightforward as you would expect, except for one entry that appears every quarter. Sally has done a bit of digging on this and was on to the financial crimes unit in Dublin. They gave her a contact in the States, and as soon as they get to work she's going to phone through and see what we can get on the dollar payments."

Flynn piped up, "And I suppose you and Sally will have to go to New York for a few days to follow it up," he said, causing a ripple of laughter around the room.

"Well, if everyone else is too busy, I guess we might have to," O'Connor responded. "Then there's the death of Paddy O'Shaughnessy's brother. We looked it up on RIP.IE. Nothing odd about that. He died in an old folks' home in Cork last year. The notice said 'Donal O'Shaughnessy, quietly after a short illness, sadly missed by his brother Patrick, son Ciaran and daughter Caoimhe, may he rest in peace'."

"We have to work on that then, but let's press on. Eamon, what have you got for us?"

Flynn recounted his expedition to Limerick, and the long interview with the Morrissey brothers. When he had finished, Hays asked, "What's your feeling about those two, Eamon?"

"Well they're a pretty rough pair, that's for sure. But strangely I think their story holds up, or more or less. They may have helped themselves to a bit more of Paddy's stuff than they are letting on, I think they torched the house for money."

"Have they collected yet?"

"Yes. The money was left in their local boozer the day after they got back to Limerick. They destroyed the envelope, so we can't get anything there. Dineen collected about three hundred that they had left, but it's all in used twenties, so no use to us, I'm afraid."

Hays made a mental note to phone Pat Dineen after the briefing to see if there was anything more to it. Dineen was a very experienced Garda, and he may have read more into what the two lads said than Flynn had recorded.

"Here are the things we need to get on with today, then. Firstly, John, can you follow up on Paddy's brother's will? Get onto the probate office and get a copy of the entire file faxed down to us. I want to know who the beneficiaries were and how much he left. Then see if you can track down the son and daughter. Get addresses for them if you can."

"Eamon, you did good work in Limerick. That phone number could be very useful. Get on to Meteor and find out as much as you can about it. Where it was bought, how long ago – you know the drill," he said. "Have you tried calling it?"

"Yes, boss. It's disconnected, but let's see what Meteor say."

"Oh, and John, can you get Sally to pursue the dollar payments. I have a feeling that's important."

"Maureen, can you come with me. I have a few things that we need to attend to."

* * *

Back in his office, Hays said to Lyons, "I'm going to call Pat Dineen in Limerick. I want to see how he thought Eamon did and check on what charges they are going to bring against the two heroes. Can you get back onto Neville Watson at the bank in Westport? Put a bit of heat on him, I think there's more than he told us, especially about the U.S. connection."

"Yes, sure, but I hope I don't have to drive all the way out there again, boss, it's an awful trek."

"And what's the story on Jerome Kelly? We need an address so we can go and interview him. If we don't have that, we'll have to phone him and pretend we want to invest some money with him, which I don't like, 'cos it smells of entrapment."

"I'll see how Sally is getting on with that," she said, and left the room.

* * *

Hays got Pat Dineen on the phone within a few minutes.

"Morning, Pat. How goes it? I hear you had a late night last night."

"Ah we're well used to it here, Mick, nothing unusual," Dineen replied.

"I was just calling to see how you thought Eamon Flynn handled himself with the two smart arses?"

"You have no worries there, Mick. He's very tenacious. I was starting to feel sorry for the two scum bags by the time he'd finished."

"Glad to hear it. Do you think he missed anything?"

"We removed O'Shaughnessy's bank card from the elder brother. I don't think Eamon knows that. That shows they were in the house before they burnt it down, I suppose. But other than that, I don't think there's anything," Dineen said.

"What are you charging them with?"

"Car theft and arson for now, unless something else comes to light. I want them put away for at least six months, keep the little toe rags off my streets for a while."

"Will they get bail?" Hays asked.

"Oh yes, they will. And we'll probably encounter them again before they go to trial. They are fairly regular customers of ours," he said with a sigh.

"Thanks very much for all your help with this, Pat. It's really appreciated. And thanks for keeping an eye on Flynn," Hays added.

"No worries, Mick, he's a grand lad. All the best." Dineen hung up.

* * *

Maureen Lyons waited patiently until ten o'clock when the bank in Westport started manning the phones with something other than a banal recorded message. At five past ten she got through to a human and a couple of minutes later Neville Watson picked up.

"Watson," he said.

"Good morning, Mr Watson, this is Detective Sergeant Maureen Lyons from Galway. You may remember we met a few days ago in your office," she said in a business-like manner.

"Oh yes, hello Sergeant, how can I help you today?"

"I'm just checking to see if you have any more information about Mr O'Shaughnessy's account for us?" she asked.

"No, I'm afraid not. Had you anything particular in mind?"

"Well we're curious about the US dollar payments he received. Have you any information about the source of those funds?"

"None at all. You see all that is handled electronically these days. We're just at the end of a very long train of electronic messages," he said, as if he was explaining the workings of a bicycle to a child.

"But surely you must be able to tell where the money is coming from?" Lyons pressed on.

"I can say that our correspondent bank in the States is J.P. Morgan, so it will have come through them, but beyond that I can't say. We don't get any information about the actual sender," he replied, as if the very thought of such a thing was ridiculous.

"And who could I contact in J.P. Morgan to help identify the source?"

"Really, Sergeant, I have no idea. They have over sixty thousand employees, and I have never spoken to as much as one of them. In any case, the account of origin is most likely not even held there. They just act as a conduit for moving the money."

"The inspector is not going to be very happy when I tell him this, Mr Watson. He's already muttering about obstructing the Gardaí in the execution of their duties."

"Well, there is one thing. I have been on to head office, and they have given me permission to share something with you."

"And what would that be?" Lyons asked, rolling her eyes to heaven.

"Mr O'Shaughnessy left an envelope here in our care. It's a large white envelope with his name on the front, and it's sealed with sticky tape."

"Good God! Why didn't you tell us this earlier, Mr Watson, the day we called to your office?" she barked down the phone, struggling to keep her temper.

"We have certain procedures that must be followed, Sergeant. We can't go giving out customers' property to just anyone, you know."

"Mr Watson, your customer was murdered, and not in a very pleasant way may I remind you. We are trying to bring his killer to justice, so can I ask you to open Mr O'Shaughnessy's envelope and tell me what it contains?"

"I'm sorry, that's totally out of the question. Head office have said that I may hand the envelope to a senior officer provided I get a receipt, but I'll not open it, it would be more than my job is worth."

Jobsworth is right, thought Lyons.

"Very well, Mr Watson, we will have it collected as soon as it can be arranged. Goodbye." Lyons slammed the phone down.

* * *

When the team met back at five o'clock on the Friday evening, there was a good deal to report. Sally Fahy had made some progress with the dollar payments into O'Shaughnessy's account. With the help of Gardaí in the fraud squad in Dublin, she had been able to trace the payments back as far as a brokerage in Boston called 'Irish Catholic Investments' and a quick web search revealed that they specialized in investing money for American Irish who had done well.

Hays said, "On Monday afternoon give them a call and see what you can get from them."

Lyons recounted her fractious phone call with the manager of the bank out in Westport and added a certain word that rhymed with 'banker' to show her frustration.

"Nevertheless," Hays said, "we've moved it all along nicely now. We're getting somewhere. I have a feeling the motive lies in and around those US payments, and of course the contents of the envelope," he added.

"Now, I need a drink. Why don't we go across to Doherty's – the first round is on me."

\* \* \*

Over at Doherty's Pub, the nearest decent public house, Hays and Lyons were standing at the bar organizing drinks for the team.

"Do you want me to get Westport to pick up the envelope on Monday?" Lyons asked.

"I was thinking, if you're not busy, maybe we could drive out on Sunday and stay over. Then we could get it first thing on Monday when the bank opens, and be back here by noon."

"You're on, boss," Lyons said as she looked at him with a slight grin.

"Pick me up around eleven on Sunday."

As the evening in the pub wore on, Maureen and Sally sat together and chatted. It turned out that they both had plans to do some clothes shopping in Galway on the following day, and they arranged to meet up in the shopping centre off Williamsgate Street at twelve o'clock, at the Café Express coffee shop.

As the evening went on, the team began to drift away, so by half past ten just Hays was left. A good week, he thought to himself as he strolled out into the cool night air and hailed a taxi to take him back home to Salthill.

# Chapter Seventeen

Maureen Lyons was sitting enjoying a cappuccino in the noisy little café when Sally Fahy arrived at just after twelve. Sally was dressed in well-cut denim jeans, a pink cotton top, and a grey knitted cardigan. Her hair was not in the usual ponytail, but hung loose down to her shoulders. She had just the right amount of makeup on, and Maureen thought she looked terrific.

I'll have to keep an eye on her, she thought to herself, we don't need any more complications on the team than we have already!

They chatted as they drank their coffee, and then set off around the shops to see what was on offer. By three o'clock they had accumulated six large paper carrier bags between them, emblazoned with the logos of the more expensive shops in the centre.

"I'm exhausted," complained Maureen. "Why don't we get out of here and go and get some lunch?"

"Fancy O'Connaires? I hear it's good on a Saturday." Sally said.

"Let's go."

* * *

Seated upstairs in O'Connaires, at a table by the window looking out over the docks, Maureen decided to broach the subject of careers for women in An Garda Siochána.

"Have you thought any more about joining up, Sally?" she asked.

"I have indeed. It's been on my mind constantly to be honest, but I'm not sure what to do," she said.

"Well I've been in for five years now, so I can answer any questions for you, just ask."

"Thanks. I was wondering what it's like, you know, at first."

"Pretty tricky, to be honest. Most of the men don't take girls seriously at all yet, and they can be very dismissive. When I'd finished in Templemore I came here and at first I thought I'd made a mistake," Lyons said.

"How so?"

"There was a crusty old bugger of a sergeant here at the time. He insisted on calling me the tea girl, presumably a hilarious play on my surname in his view. He was always sidling up to me saying, 'go on love, get's a cup of tea, will ya?' It wasn't just that either. There were loads of sexist remarks, some of it quite nasty."

"What sort of things?"

"If you were a bit grumpy, it was your 'time of the month' and they'd say, 'forgot your knitting again Lyons?' that sort of thing. It can get to you after a while."

"What did you do?"

"I was fed up with this sergeant, so one day when the office was crowded, and he came over to me with his usual request for tea, I stood up and said very loudly, 'I'm not your love, Sergeant, and I'm not the bloody tea girl either. Get your own fucking tea, and while you're at it, mine's a little milk and no sugar!'"

"Jesus. And you survived?" Sally asked.

"Not only that, but the following day I was at my desk and the same old devil comes sidling over and puts a mug of tea down beside me and slinks off without a word."

"Christ! Well done you. Did things change after that?"

"A bit, but it wasn't until I snagged the armed robber on Eyre Square that I really got some respect. Things changed a lot after that, and then they made me up to sergeant, and I never looked back."

"I've noticed you don't talk down to John or Eamon, or even me, at all."

"Why should I? You guys are just good cops who haven't been promoted yet. Everyone does their job, and everyone contributes. That doesn't mean that I wouldn't give out a good bollocking if someone screws up, but I wouldn't hold onto it. Mick wouldn't tolerate any skivers on the team. He's seen more than one or two of them off in his time."

"What happened to them?"

"They'll be on night shift in Dingle or Buncrana for the rest of their lives," she said, and they both laughed out loud.

"Do you think you might go for it?" Maureen asked as they tucked into fruit crumble and ice cream.

"Yeah, I think I will. Sure I can always drop out if it's too horrible, but you seem to have made a go of it, so why shouldn't I?"

"Things are changing too. Slowly, but they are changing. Lots of girls have done really well in the force. We have quite a few inspectors that are women now, and even a few superintendents. And of course, you have your pick of hunky guys with fairly good prospects," Maureen said with a twinkle in her eyes.

"I haven't seen too many of those yet!" she said, grimacing.

"John's a nice guy. Maybe not exactly Brad Pitt, but he's OK don't ya think?"

"Not my type, I'm afraid. Sure, nice enough, maybe too nice," Sally said.

"Talking of which, is there something going on between you and the boss?"

"What makes you say that? Has anyone said anything?"

"No, not a word. But if I'm going to be a detective…"

"Don't go there, hun," Maureen said, "that's private stuff."

Maureen paid the bill for the two of them, and back out on the street, both being shopped out, as it were, they parted company. They both agreed that they had enjoyed the day, and vowed to do it again soon. "But the next time," Sally insisted, "it's my treat."

# Chapter Eighteen

Hays collected Maureen at quarter past eleven on Sunday, as arranged, for their drive to Westport. Maureen was togged out in some of the new clothes that she had bought with Sally and looked really good. He told her so when she got into the car, and was rewarded with a soft lingering kiss that set the mood for the trip ahead.

It was a bright spring morning as they drove out on the Headford road with the sun high in the sky and just a few cotton wool clouds. When they reached Headford, Hays decided to cut left towards Cong and Clonbur, skirting the shores of Lough Mask, glistening with the reflection of the sun on its calm waters. From there, they tracked across the narrow winding road to Finny, finally making their way to Leenaun. By this time the pair were decidedly peckish, and stopped at the Blackberry Restaurant where the road meets the main N59, for lunch.

When they had ordered their meal, Hays asked Maureen how she had got on with Sally on their shopping trip.

"I think she might be up for joining the force. She has some misgivings, and I didn't hold back on some of the issues she could face as a pretty young girl when she starts out."

"I bet you didn't," Hays said smiling, "but you didn't manage to put her off?"

"No, not at all. I think she's quite keen. Would you be able to help her if she did decide to go for it?"

"I don't think I could do much for her as far as Templemore is concerned, though you could drop in on her from time to time to see how she's getting on," he said.

"Oh right, so she's my charge now then, is she?" Maureen replied rather snappily.

"No, it's not that. It's just that getting a visit from a crusty old inspector when she's being trained might not do her career a lot of good."

"You're right there," Maureen said, softening, "I'm sure I could keep in touch. What about after Templemore?"

"That's easier. I can line up a slot for her in Mill Street. She'd be uniformed for a year or two, but after that we could probably convert her to her own clothes."

"Do you fancy her?" Maureen asked, looking intently at her boss for a reaction on his face or in his eyes.

Hays put his hand over Maureen's on the table. "She's a pretty girl, no mistake, but I think one sassy little female detective is enough to keep me fully occupied, don't you?"

"That's not an answer," she said, stroking the back of his hand with her thumb, "but I suppose it's as much as I'm going to get."

"For now," he said.

\* \* \*

After lunch they set off again towards Westport, choosing the scenic route that took them through the hills to Louisburgh. The scenery was breath-taking, and there was almost no traffic, which was just as well because the road narrowed to a single car's width in places. When they reached Louisburgh, they turned right through Lecanvy along the rugged Atlantic coast into Westport.

Westport had benefitted from the construction of several new hotels during the Celtic Tiger years. Although some of them had got into severe difficulty after the financial crash of 2008, they had managed to stay open. Now, in steadier times, they offered good value and excellent facilities to the tired traveller.

The Knockranny House Hotel was one such establishment. Maureen had secured a good dinner, bed and breakfast deal, and when they checked in, they were delighted to be allocated a superior room with a gorgeous view of the mountains.

The dinner exceeded both their expectations. "A good choice," Maureen said to herself as she polished off a rather large portion of pavlova.

They spent a close and exquisite night in the huge king-sized bed, all thoughts of Sally Fahy and the case they were working on banished from their minds.

They rose at eight o'clock and enjoyed a hearty breakfast before checking out and making their way back to the town centre which seemed to be largely still asleep at that early hour on a Monday morning. At half-past nine they rang the doorbell at the bank, hoping that Mr Watson would be at work thirty minutes before the bank's official opening time. After a few minutes the door was opened a few inches by a dark-haired girl in a bank uniform, who peeped out and said, "The bank isn't open yet. Come back after ten."

Hays held up his warrant card in front of the girl's face and said, "We're here to see Mr Watson on official business, may we come in please?" The door opened another few inches and the girl looked out to the street nervously.

"You'd better come in then," she said, admitting Hays and Lyons, and closing the door quickly behind them, and resetting several locks.

Neville Watson was in the same dingy little office wearing the same drab suit as he had been during their previous visit.

"See you've brought the heavy mob with you today," he said, instantly provoking Hays who was not well disposed towards the man in any case, based on their previous encounter.

"I hope there'll be no need for that," said Hays, "we are just here to collect Paddy O'Shaughnessy's envelope, Mr Watson. I presume you have it here?"

"It's in the safe, Inspector, which is just about to be opened right now," he said, looking at his watch. "It's on a time lock you see, and it gets released fifteen minutes before opening time to allow us to stock the cashiers."

"If you could just get the envelope for us please, Mr Watson," Lyons said.

The manager rose from his chair and navigated past the two seated detectives, leaving the room without a word. When he was gone, Lyons looked at Hays.

"What a miserable little prick!"

Hays frowned and made a hush gesture with his finger. He had the feeling the room might have had a listening device.

Watson re-entered the room carrying a large white envelope. When he was seated again behind the scruffy desk, he slid the envelope across to Hays.

"I shall need a receipt for that – head office were most insistent," he said.

Hays produced a large plastic evidence bag from his coat pocket and inserted the envelope carefully into it.

Lyons had already made out a 'Receipt of Goods' sheet and unfolded it, placing it on the desk in front of Watson. He studied it briefly.

"That seems to be in order," he said, and then looking at what Hays was doing, he asked, "aren't you going to open it then?"

"Indeed we are, Mr Watson. We'll open it when we get back to Galway and our forensic team have gone over it carefully. This may be evidence in a murder enquiry. How long have you had it?"

"A few years I think, but I can't remember every item that we are given for safe keeping individually."

"Of course not. But I'm sure you issued Mr O'Shaughnessy with a receipt when he deposited it. I'd like to have a copy please," Hays said, looking the startled manager dead in the eye.

"Well, yes, I suppose we did, but that could be years ago."

"Nevertheless, I'm sure head office would like to know that you keep impeccable records. Would you mind getting me a copy of the receipt now please?"

"That's out of the question. It could take days to locate it, and we're short staffed this week as it is," Watson blustered.

"I like to be reasonable, Mr Watson. Let's say you have the receipt delivered to me at Mill Street Garda station in Galway by five o'clock on Wednesday of this week, shall we?" Watson said nothing, so Hays went on, "otherwise we'll have to take it up with your head office."

Hays and Lyons stood up and left the room.

When they got back to Hays' car, parked a little way along the South Mall, Lyons burst out laughing.

"You bastard, Mick Hays!"

"Well he's an annoying little shit, you have to agree."

"I could hardly keep a straight face. He was squirming like an eel!"

"Good enough for him. For God's sake don't let me forget to look for the receipt on Wednesday."

"Do we really need it?"

"No, of course not. We have the envelope, that's all that counts. We don't need the receipt at all."

More laughter.

"Let's see what's in it then," Hays said, handing the evidence bag to Lyons.

"What? Now!" she asked.

"Don't tell me you believed all that bullshit about forensics. But I'm damn sure I wasn't going to give Watson the satisfaction of knowing what was in there."

"You're bad, Mick Hays, very bad," she said, opening the envelope and withdrawing the single sheet of cream paper it contained.

"It's a shares certificate in Paddy's name. The Coca Cola Company, 3,700 ordinary shares, issued in October 1967."

"There you are. There's your motive for the killing. Now all we need to do is find the killer."

# Chapter Nineteen

It was approaching a quarter to twelve when Hays and Lyons got back to the Garda station, and Hays asked Sally to arrange a briefing for twelve-thirty.

When the team was assembled, Hays started with their visit to the bank in Westport. He showed them the shares certificate that Watson had reluctantly handed over.

"Sally, can you look up today's share price for Coca Cola and see what 3,700 shares are worth in today's money? A pretty penny, I dare say."

"Now," he said, "have we any information on Paddy's brother's will?"

"I'm getting a copy of the file emailed to me this morning from the probate office in Dublin, boss," said John O'Connor. "They were pretty helpful. There were just two beneficiaries, his son and daughter. Their addresses will be in the file, but it looks like the daughter lives in Scotland."

"What was the entire estate worth?" Lyons asked.

"Just over 400,000 it seems," O'Connor said.

"So, after taxes, Donal's kids would have got, let's see, about a 150,000 each. Not bad. Do we know how it was made up?" she asked.

"Not until we get the file, so I'll know later on today. And Sally, you're going to contact that crowd in Boston when they arrive at work, aren't you?" Hays asked.

"Yes, boss, I reckon around two o'clock should do it," she said. "I have an address for that QFA guy, Jerome Kelly. He lives in a small house on the Shantalla Road. Not at all what you'd expect for a high flyer in financial services. I looked it up on Google Earth. It's a terraced house with a bright yellow door."

"Excellent, well done," Lyons said.

"Right. Well let's meet back at four and see what we have by then," Hays concluded, dismissing them.

* * *

At ten past two, Sally put a call through to Irish Catholic Investments in Boston. She was put through to a Mr Bob Jefferson. She explained who she was, "I'm with the police in Galway in the west of Ireland, Mr Jefferson. We're looking into the death of a Mr Paddy O'Shaughnessy who had some dealings with your firm. I wonder if you could tell me anything about that, please?"

"Hold on a second till I get the records up here on my PC. I know Galway a bit. My grandmother was from Athenry. Oh yes, here it is. Mr O'Shaughnessy, here we are. Well I can see we send him his dividends on his Coca Cola shares every quarter. Let's see, what else. Well he changed his bank and his postal address about eight years ago, he's now in Derry… Eh Derrygim…"

"Derrygimlagh," Sally helped him out.

"Yes, Derrygimlagh. That's about it really. There's just one other note on the file here. Seems we had an enquiry about six weeks ago from a relative asking if the shares were still held by Paddy."

"Did you by any chance record who the enquiry was from?" Sally asked.

"Let's see, I need to dig a little deeper, just a moment. Ah, here it is, yes, it was a Ciaran O'Shaughnessy. I hope that helps?"

"Yes, thank you, that's a big help, Mr Jefferson. All the best."

\* \* \*

Sally was the first to provide an update. She told the team that she had validated the payments in US dollars into Paddy's account, and that they were dividend payments from the Coca Cola shares. She also told them about the enquiry from Ciaran O'Shaughnessy.

John O'Connor had received the file from the probate office. Donal O'Shaughnessy had died of natural causes in the hospital in Cork according to the death certificate. He left a house valued at 220,000 euro, some cash, and 3,700 Coca Cola shares. Probate had been granted last October, and the funds had been disbursed in November.

"Right," Hays said when the information had been shared, "Eamon, can you get onto your new best friend in Limerick and see what's happening with Torchy and his mate? I'm not bothered one way or the other, but it's a loose end we need to tie up."

"And as for you and me, Sergeant, we'd better hit the road again. I'm starting to get interested in this Ciaran guy."

"Can we leave it till the morning, boss?" Lyons asked.

"Yeah, sure. There's no rush. But I'd like to surprise him. Sally, can you phone his place of work and just say you have a delivery for him that has to be signed for personally, and will he be there in the morning around eleven-thirty?"

"Sure, boss, I'll call him now."

"Where does he work, anyway?" asked Lyons.

"He has an I.T. company in Cork. He's on LinkedIn. Looks like he owns it, or at least is the MD. It's called ITOS," Sally said.

"Thanks, Sally. Just give me the address for the sat-nav, and let's know when you have confirmed that he'll be there."

"And you and I, dear Sergeant, are going house calling on the Shantalla! Mr QFA should be just about getting home by now," Hays added.

\* \* \*

The traffic in Galway at that time was merciless, so they decided it would be quicker to walk round to Kelly's. Thankfully the rain had eased off, and although the pavements were still slick, the clouds had cleared, and it was starting to look like a pleasant if cool evening.

The Shantalla Road was a terrific mixture of residential properties. Much of it had once been built and let out by the City as social housing as it was now called, but they had left significant gaps between the terraces, and these had been bought by property developers who had built larger, mostly detached houses in the spaces, and had no difficulty selling them, given the road's proximity to the city centre. There were also some very old workmen's cottages, arranged in terraces along the road, dating back to the nineteenth century. These were very modest dwellings, but solid all the same, if inclined to a bit of damp.

The social housing had been sold off by the city in the 1980s as the council didn't want to spend ever increasing amounts on repairs. They had been eagerly purchased, mostly by the occupants who were provided with very soft loans for the transaction, and several had opened up the small front garden to allow for off street parking, a luxury not required by the original occupants who would not have been able to afford a car.

Number seventy-four, sporting its bright yellow door as described by Sally, was in the centre of a block of four of the old social houses. It was in reasonable order, but the owner had not upgraded the windows to PVC or aluminium, as many of the others had done, and the brown paint on the frames was peeling nicely. This house still had its tiny front garden, which was unkempt, with long straggly grass and weeds growing up through the broken concrete path.

"Sally was right, very down at heel for a QFA. Let's see if he's in," Lyons said.

The doorbell was obviously not functioning, so they knocked on the glass panelled door, and stood back. After a moment they could see the shape of a person advancing down the narrow hallway towards the door, and it was opened by a thin man of about forty-five years with an open necked shirt, no tie, and crumpled navy trousers.

"Mr Kelly?" enquired Hays.

"Yes, that's me. Who are you?"

"I'm Inspector Hays from Galway Detective Unit, and this is my sergeant, Sergeant Lyons. May we come in?"

"Well it's not very convenient, I'm just about to have my tea." The man paused for a moment, and then relented, "But if you must." He turned away and walked back down the narrow corridor to the kitchen which was at the back of the house. Hays and Lyons followed.

The kitchen was old, very untidy, and none too clean. The small table was festooned with dirty crockery and cutlery, and in the centre there was an open Domino's pizza box, with one triangular wedge already removed. A bottle of beer stood beside it.

"Sorry to disturb you, Mr Kelly, we won't take much of your time," Hays said, not meaning a word of it.

"So, what line of business are you in then?" he went on.

"I'm a financial advisor, investments, pensions, that sort of thing."

"A QFA, qualified financial advisor, isn't that it?"

"Yes, that's it. Why do you ask?"

"Well, not to delay you too much, Mr Kelly, we're investigating the death of a man out in Connemara. Sad case really, he was very old and lived alone near the Alcock and Brown memorial. Do you know it at all?" Lyons said.

"Well, I know the area a little. I have a few clients out that way. Devil of a place to get to. It takes me all day to do the trip, and I'm usually wasting my time."

"And do you know the man we're talking about? His name was Mr O'Shaughnessy. Maybe he was one of your clients?" Lyons went on.

"O'Shaughnessy, no, I don't think so. But I meet lots of people in this line of work. That's what my job is all about. I may have met him at some stage. Why, what's the story?"

"That's it you see, one of your leaflets was found at his house," Hays said, and let the sentence hang.

"That's perfectly possible. I may have called on him at some time, who knows? But he's not, or wasn't, I should say, a client."

"Do you have dealings with many of the old bachelors living out in the west, Mr Kelly?" Lyons asked.

"As a matter of fact, I do. They're nearly all small ticket items – you know, a life policy worth a couple of thousand to pay for their funerals. Some of them have a few bob saved, and want to get a better return than just putting it in the bank, but that's unusual. It's hardly worth my while servicing the area really, but it's a nice drive when the weather is fine, and I get fed up pounding the city streets."

"So, when would you have been out there last?" Hays pressed on.

"Let me see, about three or four weeks ago I think. I'm due back out there to finish out a few deals in Clifden next week, so yes, it would be about four weeks ago."

"Do you keep a diary, Mr Kelly?" Lyons asked.

"Yes, of course. Why?"

"May we see it, please?" she asked.

"Now look here, what's all this about? I've told you I didn't know this Paddy O'Shaughnessy bloke. I don't know how he got to have one of my leaflets – maybe a friend gave it to him, or maybe I did call on him, but that's it. Can you leave me alone now please? My tea is getting cold."

"Very well, Mr Kelly. But I'd like you to produce a full list of all your clients for us and hand it and a copy of your diary in to Mill Street Garda station before 6 p.m.

tomorrow evening for my attention," Hays said, handing the man his business card.

"Good God, Inspector, as if I haven't enough to be doing. Very well, I'll do it, but I don't see the point."

"Thank you, Mr Kelly, we'll leave you to your meal then," Hays said.

\* \* \*

Back outside, Lyons said to Hays, "Well what do you think of our Mr Kelly?"

"Not much. He didn't correct us about the QFA thing, and how come he knew O'Shaughnessy's first name? Neither of us mentioned it."

"Yes, I picked that up. There's more to him than it seems. I think I'll get Sally to do a root and branch check up on him tomorrow and see what we can find. I bet he rips off those poor old men out in the west – funeral policies my eye!" she said.

"And what about his car, did you clock the reg number?"

"Yes of course I did, I have it written down. I presume it was that none too fresh Peugeot parked half way up on the footpath outside his house with the out of date NCT and bald tyres."

"That's the one. There was a Peugeot key on the draining board in his kitchen. If he is ripping off the old timers he's not splashing it about, is he?" Hays replied.

"No, he's not. But that could be all part of the master plan. We've seen that before. Do you fancy him for it?" she asked.

"I can't see why he'd beat up and kill O'Shaughnessy, unless Paddy had let it slip that he was sitting on a fortune in Coca Cola shares, which I doubt. But let's wait and see."

# Chapter Twenty

ITOS occupied a unit on the Hollymount industrial estate in Hollyhill, County Cork. It was a grey, soulless building with a cracked concrete apron outside where four car spaces were painted in large white letters with the company name.

Hays had set off with Maureen Lyons from her house at eight o'clock, and with the traffic around Galway, and having to go via Limerick, it had taken them over three hours to reach their destination. When they arrived in Cork they were both gasping for a coffee. They sought out a small independent coffee shop and had an americano apiece.

ITOS didn't really have a reception area. Inside the front door there was an unoccupied desk with an electric doorbell screwed into the top and a typed note saying, 'Ring for service'.

Lyons pressed the bell and they waited.

After a couple of minutes, an inner door opened, and a young guy in scruffy denim jeans and a black T-shirt came into the hall. Hays introduced them, and told him that they were there to see Ciaran O'Shaughnessy.

"I'll see if he's in, hold on there a minute," the young man said. Before he could escape back to whatever lay behind the inner door, Hays asked, "What kind of car does he drive?"

"A blue BMW three series," replied the young man.

"Then he's in," Hays said.

The young man disappeared, and the inner door closed with a sharp thud.

"Shades of the bank," said Lyons.

"Exactly, and I'm in no humour to be pissed about after that drive."

Lyons looked around the small vestibule for some indication of what ITOS actually did. Usually such areas were covered with posters extolling the virtues of whatever services the company provided, but not in this case. The walls were totally bare.

Just as they were becoming impatient, the inner door opened again, and a man in his mid-forties appeared. He was roughly five foot nine inches in height, chunky, rather than overweight, with dark receding hair and a sizeable bald patch on the crown of his head. He was dressed in a black suit that was somewhat crumpled, and a pale yellow shirt with a button-down collar.

"Brown shoes," Lyons thought to herself, and wasn't disappointed.

"Inspector, Sergeant, how can I help?"

"Mr O'Shaughnessy, I presume? We'd like to have a chat with you, please. May we use your office?" Hays enquired.

"I'm sorry, much of our work here is highly confidential. We can't admit the public beyond this area," O'Shaughnessy replied, using a little speech that appeared to be well rehearsed.

"OK, Mr O'Shaughnessy, I guess we'll have to adjourn to Anglesea Street Garda station then, we're not so fussy, we entertain all sorts there."

"Perhaps on this occasion it's OK to bring members of the force inside. Follow me."

O'Shaughnessy's office was located up a flight of steel stairs. On the way, they saw a number of metal cages, each one packed with stacks of black Dell servers with flickering green lights. An electronic hum filled the space, fighting with the noise of two large air conditioning units that were struggling to keep the temperature down to manageable levels.

The office was cramped and untidy, but not especially small. There was a desk, several chairs, and two white bookcases against the walls standing about a metre high. The tops of the bookcases were cluttered with bits and pieces of equipment and parts. O'Shaughnessy's desk was untidy, covered in what appeared to be stacks of jumbled up papers. The single window, dirty and barred on the outside, was to the side of the desk and behind it. A bare fluorescent tube lit the room.

When they had taken their seats, Lyons began the proceedings.

"Mr O'Shaughnessy, as I'm sure you know, your uncle Paddy O'Shaughnessy died suddenly at his home in Derrygimlagh recently. We're looking into the matter and wonder if you could tell us something about the man, his background, his past, you know, that sort of thing?"

"I'm not sure how much I can tell you. We weren't close, not close at all. I think the last time I saw uncle Paddy was at dad's funeral last year."

"Were they close, your father and Paddy?" Lyons asked.

"Yes. They certainly had been. Of course, they had grown apart more recently when Paddy stopped driving. It's not easy to get from here to Connemara, you know."

"It seems that both your father and his brother were in possession of a quantity of Coca Cola shares. Do you know how that came about?" she asked.

"Oh that. I didn't know Paddy had them too," he said, "but the two of them worked for an uncle in Sligo years ago. He had a pub, and he gave them both a job after they had finished school. For some reason, the uncle gave my father a hundred dollars' worth of Coca Cola shares as a leaving present. They were only worth a few quid then. I didn't know he had given Paddy some as well, but it stands to reason."

"Did you inherit your father's shares?" Hays asked.

"Yes, well, sort of. They were sold, and the proceeds split between Caoimhe and me."

"How much did they fetch?" Lyons asked.

"I'm not sure, to be honest. Quite a bit though, I was surprised. Why the interest, anyway?"

"Was your sister in touch with Paddy to your knowledge?" Lyons asked.

"Oh no. To be honest, she doesn't bother with any of us since she moved to Scotland. But of course she came back for Dad's funeral, just for the day."

"Can you think of anyone who would have wished your uncle harm, Mr O'Shaughnessy?" she asked.

"Good God, no of course not. Why, what do you mean?"

"Just making enquiries. There are certain aspects of your uncle's death that are not entirely straightforward, Mr O'Shaughnessy."

"I see. Well of course if I can be of any further help," he said without finishing the sentence.

"Just one more thing, Mr O'Shaughnessy. Have you been here in Cork for the past two weeks or so?"

"Oh heavens no. I travel around a lot. Dublin, Sligo, Belfast, even Galway sometimes. Our business is well scattered."

"What exactly is it that you do here?" Lyons asked looking around the room for clues.

"I'm afraid if I told you that I'd have to kill you," he replied with a big grin. The two detectives stared back at him totally straight faced.

"Sorry. We provide network services and hosting for companies and government departments. Lots of companies don't have the expertise or the interest in running their own I.T., so we do it for them. Naturally, security is to the fore. That's what all the locked cages are about downstairs. We have to keep each client's stuff quite separate, and totally secure of course."

"Is the business doing well?" Lyons asked, getting up to leave.

"Very, thank heavens. We went through a rough patch during the crash of course, but now everything is back on track. Yes, we do very nicely."

They made their way carefully back down the metal staircase and out to the little reception room at the front. O'Shaughnessy bid them farewell and handed Hays a business card, and soon the two were back out in the open.

When they were inside the car, Hays said, "Let's get some lunch, I'm starving."

"There are some good restaurants in Blarney. Let's head out there. And I'll drive back, give you a break," Lyons said.

On the way to Blarney, Hays asked if she thought the trip had been worthwhile.

"Yes, I think so," and then she nudged his thigh and held up two plastic tie wraps in her left hand.

"Christ! Where did you get those?"

"In his office. They were on top of the bookcase."

"I must be getting old," he laughed, "I didn't see a thing!"

"Classic diversion tactic. I was fiddling with the settings on the chair, and he was looking at me thinking 'she can't even adjust the height on an office chair', when I reached behind me with my other hand and slipped them into my pocket. And yes."

"Yes what?"

"You are getting old!"

He slapped her leg playfully.

"Watch it, Lyons, or you'll be back on the beat catching bank robbers."

"At least I'll get some recognition for that!" she jeered.

They took their time over an excellent lunch in Blarney, and Lyons drove them back to Galway. They hit the city traffic just at the start of the rush hour, and the road in from Oranmore was clogged with slow moving vehicles. They got back to the station just after five o'clock, but decided it was too late for another meeting with the team, and that it would all keep till the morning in any case.

# Chapter Twenty-one

The team had all arrived by nine o'clock on Wednesday, so Hays decided to have their briefing without delay. It was a miserable day in the city, with incessant heavy rain lashing the streets and thick grey clouds overhead. The team seemed to be as glum as the weather as Hays outlined the trip to Cork and their meeting with Paddy O'Shaughnessy's nephew.

"So, where does all that leave us?" Eamon Flynn asked.

"Well, we know O'Shaughnessy hasn't been completely open with us. He said nothing about his call to Boston, and even feigned surprise that Paddy had Coca Cola shares, which he already knew. It may be innocent enough, but it needs to be checked out."

"John, can you get those two tie wraps over to forensics? I'd like to see if they are the same brand that we found on Paddy," Lyons said, holding them up in a clear evidence bag.

"And, Sally, I'd like you to do a deep dig into ITOS. I want as much detail as you can find. Accounts, press releases, client lists – everything. Who owns it, how solvent it is – the whole deal. And while you're at it, have a good snoop around on one Jerome Kelly, QFA that was – he's a bit tricky for my liking, and he wasn't entirely honest with us when we called on him. Can you do that?"

"Yes, sure, Sergeant. I'd love to. But it will take me most of the day. Is that OK?"

"Of course, Sally, however long it takes. Just make it thorough."

The team spent the rest of the day getting the case file into proper order, updating the computers with as much information as they could find, but for some reason the day dragged terribly. When the clock finally crawled round to five, Hays told them all to go home. On his way out, he stopped at the front desk and asked Sergeant Flannery if Kelly had left an envelope in for him.

"Sorry, Inspector, nothing, and I've been here all day," the sergeant said with a weary sigh.

"Damn!"

* * *

Maureen Lyons got home to her apartment down by the river Corrib at ten to six. She had stopped off along the way to buy a few ready meals, and when she had changed out of her work clothes into jeans and a T-shirt, she popped a chicken curry in the microwave to heat up. When the cooker pinged, Maureen poured herself a generous glass of red wine, and settled in front of the telly with her feet up to watch the news.

When she had finished the meal, she moved over to the table in her small lounge and logged onto her laptop computer. She opened her email which had half a dozen spam mails from various shops that she had enrolled with, and another one from an obscure address with just a single word in the subject line – O'Shaughnessy.

Curious, she opened it.

GIVE UP THE O'SHAUGHNESSY CASE. HE DIED OF OLD AGE. LEAVE IT OR YOU WILL BE SORRY. WE KNOW WHERE YOU LIVE AND WE'RE WATCHING YOU.

Maureen felt a nasty chill creeping all over her. She had never received anything like this before, and the fact that it had come through to her personal Gmail account was scary. She looked around the room, half expecting to see a villain in a hoodie hiding behind the curtains. She felt very uncomfortable, as if her own private space had been invaded.

After a few minutes, when she had checked out the flat to make sure there was no one there apart from herself, she went into the bedroom and retrieved the pay-as-you-go phone that was taped to the back of her underwear drawer. She turned it on, and mercifully it had still got some charge left in the battery. She launched the text messaging application and keyed in Hays' mobile number from memory. The message itself was just four words – "Sa bhaile, cuidiu liom" – and she pressed send. This was the Irish words for "at home, help me" and it was a protocol that Hays and herself had set up in case either of them was ever in trouble. She knew he would respond urgently, and alone, until the nature of the situation was established. Maureen knew enough not to use her normal phone for this communication. Whoever was threatening her could easily be eavesdropping, her home could even be bugged.

* * *

Fifteen minutes later Hays pulled up outside Maureen's apartment. He had a good look round, and then sounded three very short beeps on his car horn. Anyone listening would think that it was just a car alarm setting. Maureen knew the signal and pressed the door release button on her intercom to admit her colleague.

When Hays came into her apartment, he raised his index finger in front of his lips. He took a small black electronic device from his pocket, turned it on, and swept each of the rooms in turn, searching for a listening device.

"Nothing," he said, "are you OK?"

"Yes, I'm fine. Sorry for the three nines, but look at this," she said gesturing towards the open laptop on her desk. Hays read the email and let out a low whistle.

"We've hit a nerve somewhere. I wonder who is behind this?"

"The bank guy; the nephew; the QFA; someone we haven't seen yet – who knows, but it's a bit scary."

"Damn right it is. OK. Here's what we're going to do. Pack enough for three or four days and bring your toothbrush. You're coming to stay with me till we get this sorted."

"Is this how you get all your girlfriends to move in with you, Mick? So romantic!"

He walked over to her and took hold of her upper arms and kissed her forehead.

"Just looking after the team. No, but seriously, I couldn't bear it if something happened to you. You know that." He kissed her again, properly this time.

\* \* \*

Maureen had never been upstairs in Mick Hays' house out in Salthill. It was a pretty average three-bedroom semi, the main bedroom looked out to the front, and there was a half-decent view of the sea. She noticed that the place was typical of a man living on his own. It was tolerably clean, but the curtains, carpets and bed linen were old and tired looking. She settled in quickly, putting her few clothes into an empty drawer and her wash things in the bathroom. Before going back downstairs to join him, she had a quick look round for any traces of another woman, but found none.

Downstairs, they drank a couple of glasses of red wine, and Maureen finally began to relax.

"I want you to take the day off tomorrow. Drop me in and take my car. I'll bring in your laptop and we'll see if we can trace the sender of the email. Keep your main phone off. I'll contact you on the stand-by one."

"I'm not sure, Mick. Do you not think that's giving in to them a bit?"

"No. Your safety is what matters, so please don't fight me on this. I know what's best."

"Thanks," she said, and snuggled in a bit closer to him.

# Chapter Twenty-two

Lyons dropped Hays off at Mill Street at eight-thirty the following morning and drove back to the house in Salthill in his car. She hadn't showered yet, so she washed and tidied up, but by this time it was only nine-thirty and she had no idea how to fill the day.

She went back to the bedroom where they had spent the night together and looked at the bed.

"This won't do at all, Mick Hays, it's just not good enough," she said out loud to herself.

Half an hour later Maureen found herself in Eglington Square in the heart of Galway city. She made straight away for Brown Thomas and headed directly to the household linens.

Hays' bed was a standard four-foot six double, so there was lots of choice available in sheets, duvet covers and pillowcases. She browsed the linens carefully and selected two fitted sheets in cotton with a high thread count. They felt luxurious to the touch, and the assistant assured her that they were the most popular in their luxury range and would last for ten years or more.

God knows where I'll be in ten years, she thought to herself, maybe still sharing Mick Hays' bed – and maybe not!

Next, she chose a bright patterned duvet cover and a set of matching pillowcases, and then she doubled up on the purchase to ensure that it would be safe to throw Mick's current stuff away. Finally, she equipped herself with two complete sets of fluffy cotton towels. One was pale blue, and the other a rich cream colour. Each set went all the way from face cloth to bath sheet.

She left a small fortune behind her in the shop and struggled back to the car with the three enormous carrier bags. She locked all the stuff in the boot out of sight and set off again – she wasn't finished yet!

Maureen went back to Dunnes Stores and quickly found the homewares section. She spoke to a very helpful girl about curtains, not having measured the ones in the bedroom before she set out. The girl pointed Maureen to a range of ready-made curtains that she assured her would fit the window in the upstairs bedroom, and Maureen took her time browsing the various offerings before settling on a nice pale pair with a sculptured pattern. She bought them and added a couple of cushions that matched the curtains to scatter at the top of the bed.

By lunchtime, Maureen was back at the house unloading all the new purchases when Mick called her on the stand-by phone.

"How's things? Any more surprises?"

"No. How's things there?"

"We're making progress. I'll fill you in later. I just wanted to see that you were OK."

"Never better. Just sorting out a few bits and pieces. I'll see you around six. God! Listen to us, like an old married couple. Go on, will ya?"

Hays laughed and hung up.

When Maureen had taken a light lunch of soup that she had found in the fridge, she set about Mick's house with a vengeance. She changed the bed clothes, took down the old drab green curtains, and replaced them with the fresh bright ones she had bought earlier. Then she got busy with the bleach and cream cleaner and attacked the bathroom. She cleaned out all the grouting between the tiles, and down where the shower doors ran in a rail, which had become black and stained. She scrubbed the floor, putting out the new towels on the towel rail. She stood back to admire the makeover. "Christ, I hope he doesn't throw me out on my ear," she said to herself, but inwardly she felt that he would be quite pleased.

# Chapter Twenty-three

Mick Hays brought Maureen's laptop into the station with him when she dropped him off. Sally was already busy on her PC, and Eamon Flynn was at his desk.

"Morning, Sally. A bit later on when things get going, could you get on to the technical bureau in Dublin? We need a good computer guy to do some digging on an email Maureen has received."

"Sure, boss. But you know my brother is studying computers at the university here in Galway. He's pretty good at stuff like that. Would he be any help?"

"Well perhaps, but we need to get this done as quickly as we can. Do you think he might come in and have a look for us?"

"Why don't I call him and see what he's up to?" Sally said.

"Thanks. Oh, and have you found anything out about ITOS?"

"Yes. I'm just typing it up now. It makes very interesting reading!"

"We'll have a chat at twelve and you can tell us all about it. Oh, and did the front desk say there was an envelope for me?"

"No, sir, nothing."

No sooner had Hays sat down at his desk than the phone rang.

"Plunkett here, Mick. Could you pop up to me for a few minutes?"

"Of course, sir. Is now OK?"

"Yes, fine," and the superintendent put the phone down.

* * *

In Plunkett's office, Hays was invited to sit in front of the large mahogany desk.

"Just wondering how this O'Shaughnessy thing is panning out, Mick?"

"Well, we're making progress. It's tricky, because we don't know exactly when he died, and there's very little forensic evidence. But we're getting there."

"I understand you have interviewed his nephew, Ciaran."

"Yes. He's probably going to be a beneficiary of the will in due course, him and his sister."

"You need to go easy there, Mick. Your man is connected. Apparently, he does a lot of work for various TDs and even the Taoiseach."

"Have you had a call from Merrion Street?"

"The usual bullshit, carefully phrased, but basically asking us to back off."

"I think you know me better than that, Superintendent. And you should know that one of my

133

officers has received direct threats too. I'd like to see this one through, sir."

"No chance it could be put down to an old man dying of natural causes then? Get the clowns off my back?"

"Afraid not, sir, unless you're giving me a direct order to drop it?"

"You know me better than that, Mick. But be careful. I don't fancy a transfer to the Aran Islands, and you could end up back in clothes."

"Thanks. I hear what you're saying. I'll go carefully, but the very fact that someone is that rattled tells us something."

"Who was it that got threatened?"

"Sergeant Lyons. A nasty email to her personal account. Said she was being watched, and they know where she lives."

"Is she safe?"

"I have it under control, sir, she'll be fine."

* * *

At twelve o'clock they had a meeting. Hays filled them in on why Sergeant Lyons was taking the day off. Sally said that her brother would be in at around two o'clock and was looking forward to the challenge. Hays emphasised to her that the entire matter had to be kept totally confidential, and she confirmed that she had made that abundantly clear to Trevor.

Hays then asked for an update on ITOS.

Sally handed round a two-page set of typed notes.

"The company is basically broke. They have debts of over a million euro, and it seems to be getting worse every day. They are heavily bank borrowed, and there are other loans too, but I haven't found out who they are from yet.

Ciaran is the only shareholder, and he put the entire proceeds of his father's will into the company by way of a debenture."

Sally noticed the puzzled looks on the faces of Eamon Flynn and John O'Connor.

"It's a way of lending money to a company that's more secure than just putting in more shareholders' funds. A debenture holder has first call on the assets if the company is liquidated."

"And did that not solve its financial woes, Sally?" Flynn asked.

"No. It was a mere drop in the ocean, but it allowed him to keep the doors open for a few more months."

"So, let's just speculate for a minute," Hays said. "Say he knew that Paddy had over a hundred grand in Coca Cola shares. If he could have got hold of that money, he might have been able to use it to buy some more time at least."

"Yes, sir, and the shares are as good as cash. He wouldn't have had any trouble converting them into readies," Sally added.

They all remained silent for a few moments, digesting the news.

"And what about our QFA, Sally?" Hays asked.

"I'm still working on that, boss, but there have been quite a few complaints about him to the regulators. He's no longer a QFA as you know, but he still poses as one. I'm getting his phone records sent to me, although I had to pretend to be a Garda before Tesco would talk to me – I hope that's OK?" she said, looking nervous.

"Of course, that's not a problem. Let me know when you get them, and can we see if we can find out who he banks with?"

"Yes, sir, I'll see what I can do."

"Right, Eamon, your turn. What of our two clients from Limerick?"

"Clients is right. Your friend Pat Dineen got very fed up with them. He's charged them with taking and driving away, and two counts of arson and conspiracy to pervert the course of justice, and obstructing. He says he'll dream up a few more charges before he's finished. They're on remand – they didn't even ask for bail. He wants them off the streets. He says they should get two years when it comes to court."

"Excellent. Thanks, Eamon, that's cheered me up no end," Hays said, smiling. "Now, for the rest of the day I'm going to stay close to Sally's brother to see what he can get from Maureen's PC. Sally, can you keep digging into Ciaran O'Shaughnessy, see if you can find out anything more about him? If he's desperate for cash, he could be up to all sorts. Check his passport records too. Eamon, you and John had better take a look at this burglary at the Centra store that came in this morning. I think it's just the usual fags and booze, but you never know what you might turn up. And when you've done that, I want you round at Kelly's address on the Shantalla at six o'clock. Bring him in for questioning, and make sure you bring his diary, his mobile phone and his laptop with him."

# Chapter Twenty-four

Trevor Fahy arrived at Mill Street Garda station just after two o'clock. He was tall, rakishly thin, with a mop of fair, curly hair, and was dressed in the typical student's uniform of black jeans and T-shirt, and a grey zipper jacket bearing the North Face logo.

Sally brought him up to the incident room and introduced him. Then Hays asked him to come into his office where Maureen's PC was sitting on his desk. Hays again emphasised the need for total discretion and thanked the lad for coming to help.

Trevor had brought his own laptop with him too, explaining that he had a number of specialized programmes on it.

"Well at least it's Windows seven, not eight or ten," he said as he moved the touchpad on Maureen's PC bringing it to life.

"Does that make a difference?" Hays asked.

"Seven is much easier to work with. It's pretty open, and there are lots more tools to use on it. Let me just open the email and see what we've got."

"Do you think you'll be able to trace it?"

"Well certainly for a good bit back, yes. All emails leave a trail of the route that was used to get them to the ultimate recipient. But of course the sender has various ways of disguising who he or she is if they really want to. Most people don't bother though, and I can usually get behind the camouflage in any case."

Trevor opened his own laptop and started it up. He was looking at the message that had been sent to Lyons and typing furiously on his own machine.

"Hmm," he said, "this is interesting. Most emails we get here come in via New Jersey. There's a huge hub there that nearly everyone uses. But this one has come the other way, via a server in China!"

"Is that a problem?" Hays asked.

"No, not at all, it's just unusual."

"Would you like a coffee?" Hays asked, feeling a bit superfluous.

"Great, thanks. Just a drop of milk, no sugar," the young man replied. Hays went to their somewhat basic kitchen and brewed two cups of coffee. Sally came in just as the kettle boiled.

"Here, let me do that for you, sir," she said, reaching for the mugs.

"No, it's fine, Sally. Do you want one?"

"Yes please, milk, no sugar. How's he getting on?"

"Well he's got as far as China so far, so I guess that's progress!"

"Poor Sergeant Lyons. That's an awful thing to happen. Does that sort of thing crop up often?"

"Hardly ever. In fact, I can't remember it ever happening before. She's OK though. She's strong. It will take more than a nasty email to shake her."

"I know. We had a day out last Saturday, shopping and stuff. She's really nice, but I can see she could be tough too. Is that important if you're in the Gardaí?"

"Not essential, but it can be helpful if things get difficult. Are you thinking of applying?"

"Do you really think I would be any good?"

"Better than that, from what I've seen. You should," Hays said, and lifted the two cups of coffee and returned to his office.

Trevor Fahy was enjoying himself more than a little. He worked on the two laptops, and his hands were dancing from one to the other as he keyed in instructions. Hays put down his coffee beside him and asked, "How's it going?"

"This is really cool. I don't think the sender has done anything to disguise himself apart from a few very basic precautions. But the routing on the email is really weird. So far, I've traced it to China, then to Hong Kong, and then back to mainland China, and now I'm working on the next leg. Should have more in an hour or so. Thanks for the coffee."

Hays stayed in his office with the young man who rarely looked up from the two PCs. At ten to four, Sally knocked on the door and beckoned Hays out into the corridor.

"Sorry to disturb you, sir, but I've been back onto Meteor about the phone number we got from the two

Limerick lads. They say that the phone was purchased in their shop in Cork, Oliver Plunkett Street."

"Interesting. Did they say when?"

"The day before Paddy O'Shaughnessy's house burnt down."

"Nice work, Sally. Now, can you get on to our good friends in Cork. Don't tell them too much. Tell them we're sending down a crew to see if the shop has any CCTV of the day the phone was bought."

"Right, boss, I'm on it," she said, turning back towards her desk.

At just after six, Trevor Fahy brought Hays up to date on everything that he had found out about the email sent to Maureen Lyons.

"Sorry it took so long. That China stuff is hard to work with. You have to keep translating from Cantonese!"

"Thanks, Trevor, that's great. I'll see if we can dig up a few bob to pay you for your time."

"Don't worry about that, Inspector, I enjoyed it, and it's great experience."

"Well, thanks again, it's been very helpful."

When Trevor had left, Hays phoned Maureen and told her that he was leaving now and would be home shortly.

"Bring some food, I'm starving," she implored him.

"OK," he said laughing. "Chinese or Indian?"

"Just anything edible will do. Now hurry up!"

Hays was about to leave when he got a call from Eamon Flynn.

"We're round at Kelly's house, boss. Looks like he's done a bunk. The place is empty, and a neighbour said she saw him leaving with the car piled high at about two o'clock. Do you think I should break in and see what I can find?" Flynn asked.

"I think you'll find the back door of the house is either open or has been jimmied already, Eamon, if you get my drift, so you'll be investigating a burglary. Give the place a good going over. If he left in a hurry then he's probably left something of interest. Let me know if you find anything," Hays said.

"Right, boss. Catch you later."

# Chapter Twenty-five

Hays arrived back at his house forty minutes later, armed with a large carrier bag full of a 'Luxury Dinner for Two' from the Chinese take-away down the road.

When he got indoors, he handed it over and said he was going upstairs to change, and could she open a bottle of wine. Ten minutes later he reappeared, a shocked look on his face. Maureen wasn't sure how he had taken the changes he encountered upstairs. So, she asked rather tentatively, almost defiantly, "Well, what do you think?"

"It's fabulous. Really. Like a five-star hotel. You're amazing," he said, pulling her to him and giving her a hug.

"I didn't realize it had got so scruffy. And even the curtains, how did you manage that so quickly?"

"Not telling," she said.

"Well, it's clear you'll have to stay on here a bit longer. After all there's the kitchen, the lounge, and…"

Maureen punched him gently in the stomach.

"Don't push your luck, Hays. Let's eat!"

They devoured the food largely in silence and drank the bottle of wine between them.

* * *

"That's better. Us home decorators don't get time for lunch these days," Maureen said, sitting back and relaxing.

"I still can't believe what you did, it's amazing," he said, "I'll have to pay you of course, how much did it come to?"

"Don't you dare, Mick Hays. It's just a thank you for being there for me. Anyway, how do I know who's been sleeping on those old sheets of yours? And don't answer that!"

Maureen cleared away the empty cartons and put them out in the kitchen, thinking to herself, he's right you know, this place really needs freshening up. It's grubby.

Back in the lounge she asked, "Any news on the case and that stinky email?"

"I'm almost afraid to tell you," he replied.

"Why?"

"Because it's probably safe for you to go home, but I don't want you to."

"Well maybe I'm not ready to leave, not tonight anyway, so tell me."

Hays explained how Sally had volunteered her brother to trace the email, and how he had finally discovered where it had come from.

"It was sent from an internet café in Cork. The sender set up a Gmail account, sent the email, then deleted the Gmail account all within the space of about five minutes. He managed to do it without the usual Gmail authentication too."

"I wonder how he got my email address?"

"A guess, I'd say. Your email address isn't exactly rocket science."

"I'll change it after this, that's for sure."

"What do we do now?"

"Have another glass of wine."

"Idiot! You know what I mean."

"The internet place is run by Chinese, so I'll wager they have CCTV. I'm going to get it checked out. We got a break on the phone the two Limerick lads were using too. It was also sold in Cork, in the Meteor shop on Oliver Plunkett Street."

"So, all roads lead to Cork then. You know what I'm thinking?"

"I do. But it's all a bit circumstantial for my liking. Oh, and the boss tried to warn me off."

"You're kidding. Was he serious?" she asked.

"No, not really. But he's had a phone call or two from Dublin. He's a bit uncomfortable."

"I bet he is. Hope you told him where to go."

"Yes, but not in a Maureen Lyons way!"

She punched him again.

"And Mr QFA has done a runner. His house is empty, a neighbour said he left at about two o'clock fully laden. I have Eamon round there now giving it the once over. Then we'll put out a shout for him round the country, after all we have his car reg so I doubt he'll get far."

"Great. Just what we needed. I knew there was something fishy about that guy," she said.

"So, when are you sending me back to my poor lonely bachelorette pad then?" Lyons went on.

"Not tonight anyway. Let's go and road test that lovely new bed linen."

"Good idea. Home refurbishment is tiring," she said.

"Not too tiring, I hope!"

\* \* \*

It was ten o'clock when Flynn called Hays to report progress on the Kelly house. Hays told Lyons to stay very quiet while he took the call.

"Eamon, how did you get on?"

"Interesting, boss. We found a stash of stuff under the floorboards in the back bedroom. Looks like maybe cocaine or heroin – white powder in any case. And there was some cash too, about fifteen grand in used notes, wrapped in bundles of a thousand. There's quite a lot of paperwork here as well. I'm getting forensics and the drug guys out right now to get prints and all the usual."

"No wonder he scarpered. That's good work, Eamon. If you have time, do a bit of house to house – see if anyone nearby knows if he has relations or connections anywhere around, you know the ropes," Hays said.

# Chapter Twenty-six

The following morning Lyons was back at work. They had arrived separately so as not to set off the gossip machine. Hays called a team meeting as soon as they had all turned up.

"Right, folks. Thanks to Sally and her brother, we now have a lot more information." He went on to outline the details of the mobile phone, and the trace on the email.

"I need someone to go to Cork and follow up on those leads with the locals. Eamon, fancy a drive?"

"OK, boss. Can I take someone with me?" Flynn replied.

"Aw, diddum. Will you be lonely?"

A ripple of laughter went around the room.

"Well, as you always say, four eyes and ears are better than two," he replied, blushing.

"Sally, fancy a trip to the deep south to see what police work is like in the front line?"

"Sure, if you think that's OK, sir, I'd love it."

"Right then, off you go. You know what to do, Eamon. Bring back some nice video footage of our man."

* * *

The two left for the long drive to Cork. On the way, Sally called ahead to line up the local Gardaí, so as not to intrude on their patch and cause trouble.

When they had gone, Hays told Lyons and O'Connor that he was going to see the superintendent and bring him up to speed. It was looking more and more as if Ciaran O'Shaughnessy could be involved in the death of his uncle. He asked Lyons to get busy on the QFA and see if he'd been spotted anywhere.

"If necessary, elevate it to priority one – I want that little scrote back here to answer some questions as soon as possible. I don't like being pissed about by the likes of him!"

Superintendent Plunkett was not in a good mood. Hays sensed that what he was about to say would not please his boss one little bit. When he had outlined the details of what they had discovered about Paddy O'Shaughnessy's nephew, Plunkett said, "Jesus, Mick, this could be dynamite. From what you say, it's almost all circumstantial anyway. Have you any prospect of getting any hard evidence?"

"Not that I can see just now, sir, unless the CCTV comes back nice and clear."

Hays held back from telling the superintendent about the tie wraps that Lyons had lifted from the ITOS office, as strictly speaking, that was illegal and would not be admissible in court.

"OK, well let's see how it goes, but for Christ's sake be careful, Mick. If this blows up in my face there'll be very few survivors! And what about this Kelly chap?"

"Well, he's done a runner, but to be honest I doubt he killed O'Shaughnessy. He may be a bit of a con man, but I don't see him as a killer, but we're following it up all the same."

When Hays returned to his office he asked Lyons to come in for a moment.

"The Super is going nuts. He's being put under pressure. He didn't elaborate, but I can tell. Any word on the tie wraps yet? Oh, and by the way, I didn't tell him about those, so keep that little morsel to ourselves for now."

"Nothing yet, but now that you mention it, I'll get on to forensics and see what's holding them up."

The word on the tie wraps was that they were the same brand as the ones used to anchor Paddy O'Shaughnessy to his chair, but they were from a different batch. When she told Hays, he grumbled, "More circumstantial clap trap. Let's hope Eamon and Sally get something a bit more conclusive."

"Mick, do you think it was a good idea to send Sally off with Eamon?"

"If she's going to be a Garda, she'll need to be able to handle these kinds of situations. Eamon is sound. She'll not come to any harm."

"Yeah, I guess you're right. He never made a move on me anyway!"

# Chapter Twenty-seven

Eamon Flynn and Sally Fahy took almost three hours to reach the Garda station in Anglesea Street in Cork. They were expected, and having introduced themselves at the front desk, they were soon joined by Detective Garda Kevin O'Driscoll who welcomed them and treated them to a coffee apiece in the Costa Coffee across the road from the station. It was a very welcome gesture after their long drive.

"So, what's the crack with the case you're on then?" O'Driscoll asked.

Flynn explained the link to the mobile phone and the internet café, and asked O'Driscoll how he would like to play things. O'Driscoll hadn't any strong views one way or the other, but suggested that three Gardaí descending on the two shops might be a bit much, as they were small premises in any case. Sally offered to stay at the station, but the other two wouldn't hear of it, and it was agreed that the two Galway folks should head off on their own, and simply update O'Driscoll if any wrong-doing was discovered.

O'Driscoll gave them directions to the Meteor store on Oliver Plunkett Street. When they reached the shop, they asked for a manager, and Flynn showed his warrant card. Almost immediately an attractive girl in her mid-twenties with a name badge approached and introduced herself.

"I'm Mary Casey, I'm the manager here. How can I help you?"

Flynn explained the reason for the visit and asked if she by any chance had the CCTV footage from the day in question still on file.

"We should have. We normally keep the DVDs until the drawer is full, and then we throw out the older ones. Give me a few minutes and I'll see if I can locate them."

While Mary was gone to find the DVDs, Sally and Eamon browsed the phones on display.

"I wish I could afford one of these new Samsung models, they're gorgeous," Sally said, fondling the display model.

"I'm an iPhone man myself. I know they are mad expensive, but I just love them."

"Oh well, I'm due an upgrade later this year. Maybe then," she said.

Mary returned holding four DVDs in little see-through sleeves.

"I think these are the ones you're looking for. I brought the day before and the day after as well, just in case," she said, handing the DVDs to Sally.

"When you load them, three images come up. Two are of the tills and the other is taken from above the display racks. They're not high definition quality, but they're not bad," she said.

"Thanks. Do you need a receipt?" Sally asked.

"Not at all. We just bin them after a few days anyway. You're welcome to them."

"Thanks very much," Sally said, putting the DVDs into her handbag.

Next stop was the internet café on Morgan Street. The small window was crammed with cheap second-hand mobile phones, and large plastic decals advertising 'Unlock any phone €20'. Then there was a long list of places you could call from the shop, headed up with the boast 'Cheapest call rates in Cork'.

Inside, the shop was dingy and crowded. Down along the right-hand wall were five booths separated by roughly cut unpainted chipboard with a hand-written sign stuck on the outside of the first booth, 'Internet just €1 an hour'.

The place smelled of a mixture of fast food and body odour and was none too clean. There was a small counter at the front of the shop, and behind it sat an oriental man surrounded by cables, broken phones and other electronic bits and pieces. Again, Flynn showed his warrant card, and the man said in barely understandable English, "Wait. I get Susi."

When the man disappeared behind a panel to his rear, Sally nudged Flynn's arm and gestured with her head to the ceiling where a little cluster of cameras were fixed, each with a small, blinking red light.

After a short interval, Susi emerged from behind the panel. She too was oriental. She was strikingly good looking, and when she spoke, her English was near perfect.

"Hi. How can I help you?" Susi said.

Flynn went through the ritual again, adjusting the day and date to the day that Maureen Lyons had received her threatening email. Susi seemed a little put out by the request.

"We are not responsible for what the customers do on the net," she said in a defensive tone.

Sally interjected, "We just want to see if we recognize someone who was here that day. It's not going to be a problem for you."

"Please, wait a minute," Susi said and slid back behind the wooden panel like some vaudeville act.

She was back a few minutes later and had a small flash memory stick in her hand.

As she handed it to Flynn, she said, "That will be twenty euro, please, for the memory stick."

Flynn took the memory stick from her and feigned putting his hand inside his jacket, as if he was reaching for his wallet.

"I don't think so, Susi," he said, and signalled to Sally to leave the shop.

"Bloody cheek!" he muttered as they pulled the door open and exited onto the street.

Before leaving Cork, the two Galwegians had a hearty lunch at the Old Oak on Oliver Plunkett Street. Over the meal Sally gently probed Flynn about his experience as a Garda, and his move into the detective unit.

"There's a rumour going around that Lyons is going to be made up to inspector soon," he said.

"When that happens, I'll probably go for detective sergeant. I think the boss will support it."

"Yes, I heard that too. I hope it happens. She deserves it. That would be cool if you got sergeant out of it too," Sally said.

"I hope so, as long as I don't have to move away."

"Have you got lots of ties to Galway?"

"My uncle was a sergeant here. He used to call around to our house at weekends and let me wear his Garda hat when I was about seven or eight. I'd go tearing around the place arresting everyone, looking like a plonker. The hat was way too big for me!"

Sally laughed. "I bet you looked a picture. Was that what got you into the force?"

"I suppose it was part of it. I always wanted to be a Garda from when I was really young, and that was way before we had pretty young civilian staff helping us out," he said, looking at Sally and smiling.

"Ah, away with ye. Sure, we're only here to make the real cops tea!"

"Not in your case. Hays reckons you for a detective, you know."

"Do you really think so?"

"Yes. I know it. He's on a mission to build a strong team here, and he knows a good prospect when he sees one," Flynn said.

"Are you sure he's not just trying to get into my knickers?"

"Don't be daft. Sure, hasn't he got Maureen for that!" he laughed.

Sally slapped Flynn's leg. "You're awful!" she said, laughing.

The drive back to Galway was slow and frustrating. There seemed to be endless road works and slow trucks that miraculously vanished when the road ahead was clear but reappeared as soon as a series of bends arrived. It took them till nearly six to get back to Mill Street, and they decided to call it a day rather than go in and get caught up in things.

# Chapter Twenty-eight

The following morning, as soon as Hays arrived, Sally approached him with the DVDs and memory stick they had collected from the shops in Cork.

"How was Cork?" he asked.

"A long way away," she replied, smiling.

He held up the DVDs and the other item.

"Let's hope it was worth it."

"Can you and John take one each and see if we can identify our mystery customer? If you see the same person in both it would be cool, but remember they will have different clothes, as it wasn't all on the same day in both places."

"OK, boss, I'll get started as soon as John arrives."

Hays went to his office and was browsing through his emails when the phone rang.

"Inspector Hays? This is Sergeant Donal McGroarty from Donegal. I believe you're looking for a man called Jerome Kelly, is that right?"

"Good morning, Sergeant, yes that's right," Hays said, beckoning Lyons into the office as he spoke.

"We have him here for you, if you want him. He was found up in a holiday cottage in Dungloe. The folks around knew the place should have been empty at this time of year and phoned us, so we went out this morning nice and early and lifted him. What do you want me to do with him?" the sergeant asked in a soft Donegal accent.

"Any chance you could get him down here to Galway?"

"I suppose we could now. One of my men is from Loughrea, and I'm sure he'd like a trip home. Is this fella dangerous do you think?"

"I doubt it, but don't take any chances with him. And if you could send his computer and his phone with him, that would be perfect."

"We'll see what we can do, Inspector. We'll have him there by tea time."

"Terrific. Thanks very much, Sergeant."

"There you go. Let's you and I have a go at him before we hand him over to Liam in the drug squad. We'll warm him up for him!" he said to Lyons with a smile.

* * *

By lunchtime, Sally Fahy and John O'Connor were dizzy from watching the CCTV footage from the Meteor shop and the internet café, but they had a result of sorts. They had been comparing notes all along and had identified what looked like the same customer in both sets of CCTV. The trouble was that there was no clear view of his face. Either he had been careful not to be caught, knowing that the shops were recording, or he'd been lucky. The views that they had of the man were mostly from above and behind, with little other than a slightly balding pate against a head of black hair to distinguish him.

Somewhat dejected, Sally brought the results to Hays who was sitting with Lyons in his office. When they heard the news, Hays cursed out loud, but Lyons took a more up-beat stance.

"Thanks, Sally, and John too. That's not the most scintillating television you have ever watched, but well done in any case."

She went on, "Can you get a few stills printed up from the best of it, particularly where the guy looks similar in both sets of images? Oh, and make sure they are date and time stamped. Is there any point in sending these out for enhancement?"

"I don't think so, Sarge, there's no real features to be enhanced unfortunately," Sally said.

"Well, just get the stills printed up then."

When Sally had left the room, Lyons said to Hays, "What do you think?"

"I don't know, Maureen, it's all very thin. OK, so we can see a clear motive, but we can't place him at the scene. Shit! We don't even know when the poor old bugger died. And with the Super breathing down our necks, we can't just wing it – not this time."

"Why don't I get on to Julian Dodd and demand that he gives us an accurate time of death? I'll tell him we'll put him in one of his precious fridges overnight if he doesn't come across!"

"It's worth a try, I guess. Or you could just promise to have sex with him," Hays said smiling.

"I don't think so. I don't think his blood pressure could stand it." She got up to leave.

When Dodd answered the phone, and heard who it was that was calling, he said, "Ah, Sergeant. I was wondering when you would be back on. What's on your mind?"

"We need to have a good approximation of when Paddy O'Shaughnessy died. An intelligent guess will do if you haven't got any science to back it up."

"Tut tut, Sergeant, pathology is not a guessing game, it's an exact and precise science. Intelligence, yes, of course, but guessing – oh no, I leave that to you lot!"

He's getting more pompous as time goes by, she thought.

"Well, whatever," she said, not really in the mood for witty banter with the good doctor. "As it happens, you're in luck. My enthusiastic assistant was doing some work on poor Paddy to inform a thesis he's working on concerning bacteriological development in cadavers."

Get on with it you old fool, she thought.

"There's no point explaining the details to you, obviously you wouldn't understand. But his analysis shows that Mr O'Shaughnessy departed this troubled earth exactly fourteen days before he was discovered by the nurse, give or take twenty-four hours as a margin of error."

"How certain can you be, Doctor? I mean, would it stand up in court if needs be?"

"As I said, Sergeant," he said, as if he regarded Garda sergeants to be a life form not much higher on the evolutionary scale than the bacteria he was relying on, "we don't do guessing here. I would defy any defence lawyer to find an expert witness that could refute my findings."

"Excellent, Doctor. That's most helpful. Could I ask you to put all that down on paper for me and email it across?"

"Consider it done, dear lady. Now I must get on. More bodies to chop up don't you know. Goodbye."

"Some day…" she said to herself.

* * *

Lyons recounted her exchange with the doctor in the short form to Hays who was considerably cheered up by the news.

"Well done, Maureen. I always thought you had the makings of a half-decent detective in you," he said, smiling warmly.

"So, where does that leave us now?" she asked.

"Normally I'd say we have enough to give Mr Techy from Cork a tug. But given the situation, I'd better run it past Plunkett before we make a move. Let's see if he's in," he said, reaching for the phone.

He wasn't in as it happened, and wouldn't be until the following morning, so Hays left a message with his secretary to say that he needed to see the superintendent for ten minutes in the morning and left it at that.

"That actually works better, 'cos we'll have had a good go at Mr QFA before I see Plunkett. We will either have eliminated him, or found a reason to charge him."

The Donegal crew arrived as promised at five o'clock with a very dejected and exhausted looking Jerome Kelly in tow.

Hays asked Sergeant Flannery to get him some food, and at six o'clock, Hays and Lyons joined him in the interview room.

159

"Well, Mr Kelly, we meet again. Sorry to have interrupted your holiday in Donegal. Now I think you owe me your diary, your client list, and a reason why you went AWOL, don't you?" Hays asked.

"Look, I didn't have anything to do with the old guy's death. I had to get away for a while. There are some business dealings that I need to sort out, and I couldn't do it with you lot breathing down my neck, OK?" the man said.

"No, not OK," said Lyons, "would these business dealings have anything to do with the drugs we found in your back bedroom, along with a sizeable amount in cash?"

"Jesus! What were you doing in my house? Have you a warrant?"

"Don't be pathetic, Kelly. You know damn well we don't need a warrant, and you're in a lot of trouble. We'll let the drug squad deal with your little store of goodies. What I'm interested in is how you knew O'Shaughnessy's first name, when neither of us had mentioned it on the evening we dropped in on you," she said.

"Oh, all right, I may as well tell you. I did call to his house. We had a good chat – he was a nice old codger, and he was enjoying having someone to talk to. He told me he could be coming into some money, and he'd like to invest it. He said it was a good amount, so naturally I was interested. We agreed I could call back in about two weeks and he would have the details then."

"And when exactly was this, Mr Kelly?" Hays asked.

"About four weeks ago. I was going to call on him this week, but it seems I'm too late."

"And that's it? You had no further contact with Paddy O'Shaughnessy after you called to his house about four weeks ago? Is that what you're telling us?"

"Yes, yes, that's right."

"We'll need to check on your whereabouts during the week that O'Shaughnessy died. As you may have gathered, the poor man was tortured and murdered in his house, and with the tall tales you've been telling us, I may as well tell you, you are a suspect."

"Bloody hell. That's crazy. I wouldn't get very far if I was going around killing my clients, now would I? Anyway, I was out of the country that week, in Amsterdam," Kelly said.

"How do you know what week we're talking about?" Lyons asked.

"It was in the paper. I saw it and said to myself 'just my luck'. That deal could have got me out of trouble with the drugs. I owe a fair bit of money to some not very nice types."

"Why didn't you take the drugs and money we found in your house on Shantalla Road with you when you left for Donegal?" Hays asked.

"I thought it would be safer there than travelling around with it in the car. I was going to go back for it when you lot had lost interest in me."

"Can you prove you were out of the country when O'Shaughnessy was killed?" Lyons asked.

"You'll get the bookings from my laptop. I flew to Amsterdam on the Sunday, and back on the Friday, and my hotel booking is on there too. And you can check with the airline and the hotel."

"OK, well we're keeping you in overnight while all that is checked out. And then our colleagues in the drug squad would like a word."

Kelly was ushered back to a cell for the night, and Hays said he would get Sally to check Kelly's story with the airline and the hotel in Amsterdam in the morning.

"C'mon, let's get out of here. I'm taking you to dinner, young lady," he said to Lyons.

"Oh, you are, are you? What if I just want to slob out in front of the telly with a pizza?" she snapped back at him.

"Do you?"

"No, of course not. God, you're so easy to wind up sometimes. Let's go!"

# Chapter Twenty-nine

They went for a scrumptious meal at Brasserie On The Corner in the city centre, and then made their way back to Hays' house in Salthill.

When they got in, after they had settled in the lounge, Maureen said, "God, thanks, Mick, that was smashing."

"You're welcome. Would you like a brandy to wash it down? I have a nice bottle of good Spanish Magno in the cupboard."

"Yes, please. That sounds just the job," she said.

When they were sitting back sipping the drink from their Galway Crystal brandy balloons, Maureen approached the subject that both of them had been carefully avoiding all evening.

"So, what about you and me then, Mick Hays? Where to from here?"

"What indeed. Well you know you can stay on here a while if you want to. You're always welcome," he said.

"That sounds like my distant cousin trying to get rid of me when I have turned up out of the blue and been there for a week!"

"I'm sorry, Maureen. I don't mean it like that at all. What do you want to do?"

"I've thought about it a good deal. But to be honest I like my independence, Mick. I like the way we have been getting on over the past while, but I don't feel ready for any huge commitment just yet. What about you?"

"I feel the same. I think we're doing just fine. It's almost as if it shouldn't work, but it does. Maybe I'm being too careful, but I don't want to break it, whatever 'it' is."

"Right so. I'll shift back to my place tomorrow after work. I don't think I'm in any danger, except maybe in danger of getting in too deep too soon."

Mick raised his glass and touched it against hers.

"Well let's enjoy tonight then."

If it's possible to feel relief and disappointment at the same time, then both those feelings swept over Lyons as they got physically close that evening.

"Steady girl," she said to herself. "Time and place. Time and place. You've always been good at it, now don't mess this up."

# Chapter Thirty

Hays was summoned to Superintendent Plunkett's office early the following morning, soon after he arrived at the station.

"Come in, Mick, take the weight off, would you like a coffee?" asked the boss in an ebullient mood.

"Yes, please, just a drop of milk."

When Hays had the drink on the desk in front of him, the older man went on, "Well, what's been happening with the O'Shaughnessy death then? What's the latest?"

Hays explained about the CCTV from the two sites in Cork, and about the dire financial state of O'Shaughnessy's company, as well as the evidence about the plastic tie wraps. He told the superintendent that they now had a motive, possible opportunity, but as yet no means by which O'Shaughnessy himself could have killed his uncle. He also told him about the QFA, and that whilst he had lied to them about knowing O'Shaughnessy, he appeared to have an alibi for when the old man had been killed. They were still checking it out, but it looked solid enough.

"We can't place the nephew anywhere near the scene of the crime yet, although we now know the day the old man was killed. It was exactly two weeks to the day before the nurse found him."

"So, it's still all rather circumstantial?" Plunkett asked.

"It is, yes, for now. What about the intervention from Dublin? Has that quietened down any?" Hays enquired.

"It has, thank God. I put out a few discreet feelers of my own, and it seems the pols and others are distancing themselves from Ciaran O'Shaughnessy, in case you are right and it all goes tits up. But that doesn't mean they won't be back onto it like flies on manure if your man comes up clean."

"I see. How do you think we should proceed, boss?"

"Well, Mick, if it was me in your shoes, I'd get the little bugger into a small room somewhere and put the screws on him till he confessed – figuratively speaking of course. But I never said that, you understand."

"Do you think he'd go squealing to his buddies in Dublin?"

"Even if he did, I have it on good authority that it would fall on deaf ears."

"I see. Well that's very useful to know," Hays said.

"Yes, Mick, but go carefully. You know I have big ideas for this place. I want to grow a serious detective unit here that will dominate the entire Western Region. And you and your team are very much part of all that. It's the same old story. If we get a good result here, then we'll be heroes, and I'll get to do what I want. If we screw up, then they'll move me to the Aran Islands and it will be game over."

"No pressure then, sir, I see."

"Things are getting a lot more political in the force, Mick. We have to deal with a lot of stuff that we never saw before, and most of it isn't helpful. If I need to replace a squad car these days, they nearly want to have a commission of enquiry. So, let's get the right result here, eh Mick. I have every faith in you and the team, and if you need anything, let me know."

Hays drained his cup and stood up thanking Plunkett for the coffee and saying that he would keep him posted.

Back in the incident room, the team were all present and Hays lost no time in addressing them.

"I've just had a meeting with Superintendent Plunkett," he said, "and here's what we're going to do. We're going to bring young O'Shaughnessy in for questioning – some fairly aggressive questioning at that. We'll present him with the CCTV evidence, the tie wraps, his company's finances, and we'll sweat him about his whereabouts on the day of the murder."

"You're after a confession, boss," Lyons said.

"I am, and I intend to get it. Now, John, can you get on to Anglesea Street in Cork and ask them to set up the most oppressive interview room that they have? Once we're on the road we'll get them to bring him in using a squad car with lights and all. I want you and you with me," he said, indicating Lyons and Flynn, "and we play bad cop, worse cop, and nightmare from hell cop. Any questions?"

"What about Kelly?" Lyons asked.

"We'll turn him over to Liam in the drugs squad. If there's anything there for us, he'll find it and let us know. Kelly's days as a financial advisor are definitely up I'd say.

"OK. Let's get going then. John, you stay close to the phone all day. We may need some coordination from here.

And if you've nothing better to do, check out Kelly's alibi with Ryanair and his hotel. Make sure he didn't pop back mid-week to bump off the old guy. The guys at the airport should be able to tell you that from his passport scans. Maureen, will you bring the evidence, such as it is?"

"Yes, boss."

# Chapter Thirty-one

The three detectives were apprehensive about what lay ahead, but a little excited at the same time that they might actually close the case by that evening.

They made a pit stop on the outskirts of Limerick and Hays relayed the conversation that he had had with the superintendent that morning.

"We get one good shot at this, folks, and if he doesn't come across, we'll all be back in clothes writing parking tickets in Manorhamilton or Drumshanbo."

"But, sir," Flynn said, "there aren't any cars in those towns."

"Exactly my point, Eamon."

It was nearly twelve-thirty by the time they arrived in Anglesea Street Garda Station in Cork. O'Connor had called ahead, and when they had introduced themselves, the desk sergeant told them that Detective Inspector Donovan would like to see them. They all trooped up the stairs and found his office on the third floor.

"Come in folks, come in," Donovan said in a strong Cork accent, welcoming the visitors.

Introductions were made all round, and Hays and Lyons sat down leaving Flynn standing as there was no third chair.

"We have your man downstairs. Jesus, he's livid. I've rarely seen someone so agitated, and of course he's got himself a solicitor – a Mr Daniel Murphy. Seems quite a cute sort, so you may have your work cut out. One of my uniformed men will be in with you. Are you all going in together?"

"No," said Hays, "Sergeant Lyons and myself will start proceedings. It's important he sees her after the threatening email that was sent. Then we'll rotate Detective Flynn in and out. I have someone looking to see if we can get a second twenty-four hours if we need it."

"So, you're fairly sure this is your man then?" Donovan asked.

"We are, but we only have some pretty circumstantial evidence so far, so we need a confession."

"Good luck with that! Right, you'd better get moving before he starts shouting about lunch. Oh, and by the way, we got his fingerprints off him, 'for elimination purposes' as it were."

"Excellent, thanks."

\* \* \*

The interview room was as drab and oppressive as they had requested. The green walls, and the dirty window positioned high in the wall opposite the door, combined with the smell of sweat, created a unique atmosphere which was just what the detectives needed.

When Hays and Lyons entered the room, O'Shaughnessy and his solicitor were seated side by side, and the uniformed Garda from the Cork station was standing at ease by the door.

"About bloody time!" O'Shaughnessy burst out, jumping to his feet. "What the hell do you think you are doing? I have a business to run, you know."

Murphy touched his arm and made soothing gestures, asking his client to calm down, and they all took their respective seats.

Lyons read the man his rights very slowly and deliberately, staring him in the eye with a fixed gaze throughout the short speech.

"Do you require a drink of water, or tea, Mr O'Shaughnessy, or perhaps a toilet break?" she asked.

"I require to get bloody well out of here, that's what I require!" he snapped back at her.

"Very well, then we'll begin."

Lyons explained that O'Shaughnessy had not, as yet, been charged with anything, and that they were there to progress enquiries about the brutal torture and murder of O'Shaughnessy's uncle.

"Where were you, Mr O'Shaughnessy, on Wednesday afternoon two weeks ago?" Lyons asked.

"I don't bloody know, do I, I told you I travel a lot for business. I'd have to consult my diary."

"Do you have it with you?" she asked.

"Does it look like I have it with me?" he replied, spreading his hands to show that he had nothing with him.

"I thought you might keep it on your phone, Mr O'Shaughnessy, you know, along with your emails," she said, drawing out the word 'emails' and staring at him coldly.

Daniel Murphy piped up. "Could we move along please, Sergeant? My client has answered your question."

Lyons paused for a moment and turned to look at the solicitor.

"Mr Murphy, not only has your client specifically not answered my question, but he has been rude, aggressive, and offensive in failing to do so. May I propose that you advise your client to be more cooperative and less offensive, or we'll be here for a very long time indeed."

Murphy looked at his client and raised an eyebrow.

Hays had seen Lyons in this mood before, and he was glad he wasn't on the receiving end.

"So, Mr O'Shaughnessy, I'll ask again, where were you on the afternoon of Wednesday two weeks ago?"

Murphy gave his client what he thought was an imperceptible nod, which was picked up by both detectives, and O'Shaughnessy replied, "I was in my office. I had a business meeting in Limerick in the morning at eleven, and when that was over, I drove back to my office. I arrived back around two o'clock."

"Thank you, Mr O'Shaughnessy, that wasn't too difficult, was it?" she said, "and I presume that you have people that can vouch for your presence at that meeting, and for your arrival back at your premises?"

O'Shaughnessy said nothing.

"We'll take that as a yes for now then, shall we?" Lyons said.

"And can you tell us what the purpose of your meeting in Limerick was?" she continued.

Murphy interjected again. "I can't see how that's relevant to your enquiries, Sergeant."

Lyons had had enough of this. Time to put this guy in his box.

"Really, Mr Murphy. I'm very surprised that a man of your obvious legal talent can't figure that out. We believe that your client's business is in financial difficulty, Mr Murphy, and that Paddy O'Shaughnessy was murdered for financial gain. We need to establish if there is any possible connection between those two matters, so I'll ask again…"

Murphy looked at his client and shook his head ever so slightly from side to side.

"No comment," replied the man, and he sat back smugly in his chair as if the response had acquitted him of any possible wrong-doing.

The interview proceeded on the same lines for another tortuous forty minutes. At half past one, Lyons called a break for lunch, and said that food would be brought in for the solicitor and his client, and that they could use the time to consult if required. The interview would resume at two o'clock.

* * *

The detectives adjourned to a nearby office and were joined by Flynn who had procured sandwiches for them all.

"How's it going?" he asked.

"Not much so far," Lyons admitted, "that little prick Murphy is keeping him straight."

"You did a pretty good number on him, though," Hays said smiling.

"Not good enough. He's a wily little fucker," she said, between mouthfuls.

It was agreed that Flynn and Hays would resume the interview at two o'clock. Hays asked Lyons to find out what car O'Shaughnessy owned, and its registration details.

"If I remember from our last visit, it's a blue BMW three series. But I'll get the number. I suppose you want me to get onto O'Connor and see if there's anything on it?"

"Exactly," Hays replied, heading back with Flynn to the interview room.

* * *

When the interview recommenced, Daniel Murphy had a go at Hays to see if he could wrestle his client free from the clutches of the Gardaí.

"Inspector Hays, we've had a good deal of questioning now, mostly fishing on your part. Have you any substantive evidence that can link my client to your investigation? If not, we'll be leaving."

"I'm afraid that won't be possible, Mr Murphy. We've barely got started!"

Then, turning to Ciaran O'Shaughnessy, he said, "Mr O'Shaughnessy, have you ever owned a mobile phone with this number?" He showed him the number of the phone used to set up the arson attack on Paddy's cottage.

"No, I don't recognize it," O'Shaughnessy said.

"Then how do you explain this?" Hays said, showing the suspect the photo taken from the Meteor shop's CCTV footage.

"Explain what exactly, Inspector?" Daniel Murphy asked.

"Is this not a photograph of you purchasing a pay as you go mobile phone in the Meteor shop on Oliver

Plunkett Street the day before your uncle's house was burned to the ground?"

"This is a photograph of some random person who looks vaguely like my client from behind. Hardly evidence, Inspector."

"And is this not a picture of you entering an internet café to send a threatening email to a member of An Garda Siochána, Mr O'Shaughnessy?"

O'Shaughnessy made to reply, but Murphy cut in ahead of him.

"Really, Inspector, you'll have to do much better than that. Now I suggest you either charge my client with something or let him go immediately!"

Hays managed to string it out for another half hour, not wanting to yield to Murphy's demand at once, but it was clear that O'Shaughnessy was in no humour to confess to anything. They had to release him. Hays was expecting Murphy to threaten the Gardaí with all sorts of things, but to his surprise, no threat was made.

Going back in the car the mood was very glum and there were few words spoken. They dropped Flynn off at the station, and on the way out to Hays' house Maureen asked him to give her a lift back to her own apartment with her stuff. It didn't take them long to get her few belongings together, and he left her back at her flat by the river bidding her goodnight with a quick perfunctory kiss.

# Chapter Thirty-two

The next day Hays reported the progress, or lack of it, to Superintendent Plunkett. He was expecting Plunkett to be angry, but to his surprise, the senior man was quite unperturbed.

"I know it's a disappointment, Mick, but if you resort to good old-fashioned police work, you'll nail him. You're sure it's him?"

"Yes, sir, certain. What about the fallout from up above?"

"You let me worry about that. If you've rattled him enough there won't be any."

Back in the incident room Hays called the team together again.

"Anything new?" he asked, expecting to be disappointed.

John O'Connor raised his hand.

"Yes, John, what have you?" Hays asked.

"Well, firstly, Kelly's alibi holds up. Ryanair confirmed that he actually travelled on the flights he said he did, and there's no sign of him coming back mid-week either. The hotel says he was there every night he said he was, so it looks like he was telling the truth. But there's more.

"You know you asked me to check out Ciaran O'Shaughnessy's car yesterday, sir? Well I did, and it turns out he was pinged at 15:21 p.m. doing a 130 kph heading north between Gort and Galway on the day Paddy was murdered."

"Was he now. Good work, John. There can't be any mistake about this, can there?"

"No, sir. I'm getting the Gatso folks to send over the photo, but they say it's a slam dunk."

"So, he lied to us about his movements that day. Good. We're closing in."

"Yes, boss, but it's still all too circumstantial. We need more – something positive," Lyons said.

"I agree," Hays said, and thought for a minute.

"Tell you what. Why don't you and I nip out to the cottage again? We haven't been there for a while, and you have a happy knack of finding things. Remember last year when you found that boarding card in the ditch?" he said.

"Oh, that," she said.

"Might as well," Lyons said, "better than hanging around here doing nothing anyway."

\* \* \*

It was a fine spring morning as they drove out west from Galway. Beyond Oughterard the gorse was just starting to bloom, and as they passed a few of the bright yellow bushes, the heady scent of coconut wafted in through the open car windows.

The twelve pins looked magnificent in the distance, the sunshine giving them their famous blue tones. With fluffy cotton wool clouds drifting by slowly overhead, the two detectives could not help but be moved by the sheer beauty of their surroundings.

They stopped in Roundstone for an early lunch, enjoying a pair of Mrs Vaughan's legendary smoked salmon salads, sitting looking out at the glistening waters of Bertraghboy Bay.

"How did you get on being back at home last night?" Hays asked his sergeant.

"Fine. Everything was just the same." Then, unprompted, she reached across the low table and squeezed his hand, "but I missed you."

"Me too," he said stroking the back of her hand with his thumb.

"Fuck it, Mick, we'll have to sort ourselves out," she said.

"I agree. Let's get this thing behind us first. Then we'll take some time out and see what we can come up with."

"You're not messing now, are you? I'd prefer you to be straight with me."

"No, I'm not messing, Maureen. That's not me, but we need to think things out properly if it's going to work out for us."

* * *

They reached the burnt-out shell of Paddy O'Shaughnessy's old cottage about half an hour after leaving Roundstone. It looked much the same as it did the last time they were there, except there were no vehicles around, and the blue and white crime scene tape was all but gone, with just a few scraps fluttering in the breeze.

They got out of their car and deeply inhaled the pure air. The grass was starting to grow over the track leading to the old house, and a few clover plants had put out their small, pale flowers.

"What do you want to do?" Lyons asked.

"Just walk around. Get the feel of the place. Try to imagine Ciaran arriving to get his uncle to lend him money to save his business. See what comes to you," he said.

They set off in different directions walking around the site, moving the grass and clover with their feet. After a few minutes Hays shouted, "Maureen, over here!"

He was standing quite still, looking down between his feet.

"What is it?"

"Look between my feet."

Lying in the grass between Hays' two large black leather shoes, was a coin. It was partly hidden by the grass, and he had only seen it because the sun had caught it, and it briefly flashed a beam of light at him.

"Very carefully, get that into an evidence bag. Don't touch it, and don't rub the surface, just pick it up by its edges."

Maureen manoeuvred the two euro coin into a small plastic evidence bag.

"That could have been dropped by anyone, you know," she said.

"Yes, I know. But it's time we got a lucky break."

"And what are you hoping to get from it anyway?" she asked.

"I'll tell you on the way back."

"And while you're at it, I've been thinking if Ciaran drove up from Cork in his BMW, he would have needed to refuel before going back. So where would he have done that, I wonder?"

"Possibly in Clifden?"

"That's what I was thinking, and didn't the owner of that garage, what was his name, Ferris, that's it, didn't he say he had to fit CCTV at the garage because he was getting broken into so often?"

"Christ, Maureen, I think you're right. Let's head in and see what we can dig up."

\* \* \*

Out of courtesy they stopped at Clifden Garda station and found Sergeant Mulholland tucking into a cup of tea and a packet of chocolate biscuits.

"Ah, Séan, just in time. Yes, we'd love a cup of tea, thanks!" Hays said.

They explained the reason for their unexpected visit, and Mulholland quickly volunteered Jim Dolan to go to the garage and collect the CCTV footage. He said he would get Dolan to look at it, and they would let Hays know if there was anything significant. Lyons gave the sergeant the registration number and details of O'Shaughnessy's car.

When they had finished their tea and biscuits, Hays and Lyons left Clifden and headed back to Galway. When they were underway, Lyons asked, "So what's the story with the coin?"

"Ah, yes. Well, if by any chance it was dropped by Ciaran O'Shaughnessy, we may be able to get a print off it."

"You're kidding. Surely you can't get a print off a coin, so many people would have handled it," she said.

"Yes, but I was reading the UK Police Gazette the other night, sad bastard that I am. Some outfit in Leicester have a new process that can recover prints from coins and identify the last person to have handled it. It's been used a few times in cases over there already," Hays explained.

"So, that's where our two euro is headed?" Lyons asked.

"Dead right. And if Ciaran O'Shaughnessy was the last person to handle that coin, then that places him at the scene."

"Nice. Bit of a long shot though," she said.

"Let's see what Mulholland comes up with. If, by any chance, we can get him filling up in Clifden and if the coin comes through, then we would have enough to charge him."

"A lot of 'ifs'."

"Maybe. You do think he did it, don't you?"

"What I can't understand is that O'Shaughnessy would have inherited his uncle's shares and money in a few years in any case, so why try to rob him now?"

"He's desperate. His company is on skid row, he needed the money urgently. And besides, if the old man died naturally, the inheritance would have to be split between him and his sister in Scotland, so he'd only get half. And that's assuming it was left to them in the first place."

"I wonder who he's been borrowing from. I bet there's a Limerick connection there somewhere. How could we find out?" Lyons asked.

"I could ask Pat Dineen to have a sniff around and see if he can turn anything up. He probably knows who's lending money in the area. I'll give him a call later on."

By the time they reached Galway it had started to rain. The traffic was almost at a standstill, and it was after five o'clock, so Hays dropped Lyons off at her house and headed home. He had half hoped that she would invite him in, but it didn't happen.

# Chapter Thirty-three

Later that evening, at home in Salthill, Mick Hays called Pat Dineen in Limerick.

"Hi Mick, how's it going?" Dineen asked.

Hays explained that he was still working on the O'Shaughnessy case and that he was hoping to find out if Ciaran O'Shaughnessy had borrowed from money lenders in Limerick to shore up his business.

"To be honest, Mick, it's a bit of a cesspit. There's a lot of drug money sloshing around, and there's no doubt that there's some money lending going on. But we just haven't got the resources to chase everything, so we concentrate on the drug traffic and do our best to stem the flow at that end. But listen, I have a few contacts here and there that I can talk to. I'll see if I can dig up anything."

"We're closing in on him, but we need a bit more to charge him."

"I'll see what I can find out for you, but it could take a few days. I'll get back to you."

"Thanks, Pat, cheers," Hays said and hung up.

* * *

The next day at Mill Street Garda station things were getting busy again. John O'Connor was chasing down the speeding ticket that O'Shaughnessy had picked up on the Limerick to Galway road when he had told them that he was travelling south from Limerick to Cork.

Lyons was intending to follow up with Mulholland about the CCTV from the garage, but she knew there was no point in calling him before late afternoon. Things moved at a different pace out there in Clifden, and by the time they had drunk their morning tea, sauntered down to the petrol station, gossiped with Ferris about all sorts, and actually got hold of the footage, it could be close to lunch time. And sure there would be no point in starting anything till after lunch, so Lyons reckoned it could be half past two before Dolan actually started looking at the video, that is if he hadn't been called out on some urgent business, like a donkey loose on the road somewhere.

Hays knew there was no point in trying to hurry Pat Dineen along either. The task he had taken on was a tricky one, and he would have to move carefully among the Limerick underworld if he was to get any useful information. Such matters had their own pace, and it usually wasn't quick.

Lyons came into his office carrying the bag containing the two euro coin that they had found in the grass out at Derrygimlagh.

"Boss, are you sure about this? It seems like a very long shot to me," she said.

"Come in, Sergeant, take a seat, watch and learn."

Hays powered up his PC and turned the screen so that they could both see it. He launched his internet browser and typed a few words into the search bar.

The first few items to appear related to how coin collectors can remove finger smudges from proof coins – just about the exact opposite of what they were about. But a few headings down the page there was an article about how police in the UK could now recover fingerprints from coins. It was a technique developed at the University of Leicester and involved placing the coin in a solution of chemicals that attach to any exposed metal when an electric current is applied. The fingerprints, which contain traces of grease, insulate the metal from the solution, thus creating a negative image of the fingerprint. Apparently, the technique could also be used to recover DNA from the coin.

The article claimed a high confidence level for the technique, claiming an over ninety percent hit rate in controlled samples where students had allowed their fingerprints to be taken in the conventional way, and then had them compared to prints recovered from coins that they were carrying in their pockets or purses.

"See, I told you. And if I'm guessing correctly, we'll never need to satisfy a jury with this one," Hays told the sergeant who was looking on clearly impressed.

"So, can you get on to professor what's-his-name in Leicester University and see if he would be willing to help out with our coin? We can send it across with a secure courier. I'm sure he'll only be too glad to lend a hand on a real live case. What we want back is a clear print from the coin, and of course the coin itself."

"OK, boss, I'm on it. But what if the technique only works on British coins, and not on euros?" she said smiling.

"Get out of here!" he laughed and threw a rolled-up piece of waste paper at her.

* * *

Hays had been right. Lyons got through to Professor James Lattimer with remarkable ease, and after exchanging a few pleasantries, he readily agreed to carry out the tests.

He instructed Lyons to pack the coin in a plastic coin or medal container with no sponge or any organic material around it, and to send it by secure courier to him personally. He gave her the full address.

'Secure courier' meant that the item would be hand carried from A to B in a locked case, a small one in this instance, and the courier would have credentials to ensure that the case was not opened or interfered with, or scanned by x-ray which could spoil the evidence, and give a defence barrister an opportunity to cast doubt on its legitimacy. These couriers were quite often used between Ireland and the UK, and vice-versa when the police forces of both countries were cooperating on a case.

Lyons took a five euro note from her purse and asked Sally Fahy to go downtown and get two of the required plastic containers of the correct size for a two euro coin.

"Make sure it's a good fit, that's important," she instructed.

Then she got onto the superintendent's office to arrange a courier for twelve o'clock. She looked up flights from Dublin to Leicester and found that either East Midlands or Birmingham Airport was the nearest. Consulting the airline timetables out of curiosity she found that the courier could be in Leicester by about seven-thirty that evening. She phoned the professor back to see if there would be anyone available to receive and sign for the coin at that hour.

"Certainly, I'll be here myself. I rarely leave before nine anyway, and today I have to prepare a paper for an upcoming symposium, so I'll be here, no problem."

"Thanks, Professor, oh and may I ask how long the procedure takes once you have the coin in your possession?"

"It's surprisingly quick. As it's a live case as it were, it will need to be done in laboratory conditions, so I'll get Dr Andrew Kerel to actually do the test. He's fully accredited and has done several of these for the UK Police. We've had quite a few convictions now, based on this evidence. If your case comes to court, I'll gladly send you the references."

"Thank you, Professor, that's very helpful. You were saying how long it might take?" she prompted.

"Oh yes, sorry. Kerel gets in around ten in the morning usually, so I imagine we'll have a result around lunchtime tomorrow. I can email across anything we find."

"That would be terrific, thank you so much," she said.

"No trouble, Sergeant. Glad to be of help."

\* \* \*

Sally was back in the station half an hour later with one of her own two euro coins safely stowed in a little clear plastic box, and another just like it completely empty. It was a perfect fit – the coin didn't even move around inside the container.

"Thanks a million, Sally. Now could you get some tweezers and gloves, and we'll transfer the Derrygimlagh coin to the empty container. Take your coin out and throw away the box before we start, so we don't get mixed up. We don't want your thumb print coming back from Leicester tomorrow!" she said.

At exactly twelve o'clock the secure courier arrived and asked for Sergeant Lyons. Lyons was surprised to find a very attractive tall blonde girl with a mop of curly hair and an amazing figure, dressed in black from head to toe, waiting for her in reception.

"Hi. I'm Angela Byrne," she said holding out her hand, "well at least that's what it says on today's passport. You must be Sergeant Lyons."

"Call me Maureen. It always says the same on my passport! Come on up and I'll give you the item."

The two women made their way upstairs where Lyons handed over the small package together with the address and the completed S-39 form to get the courier through security.

"When do you think you'll get there? It's just that the professor will only be in his office till around nine," Lyons said.

"I'll be there long before that. Probably around seven," Angela said.

"Are you flying to East Midlands?" Lyons asked.

"Not likely. I never use EMA, they're much too inquisitive. No, it's Stansted for me with Ryanair, I'm afraid. It's not luxurious, but at least it will be on time, and it's just about two hours in a fast car after that," the girl said.

Lyons decided not to ask anything further about the courier's travel plans. She clearly knew what she was about, which was what Lyons had been out to establish in the first place.

Before she left, Angela asked, "Will there be a return trip for this?"

"Yes, but it won't be urgent. Next week will do."

"It may not even be me that gets it then, there's quite a few of us doing this."

"Do you get to go anywhere nicer than the English Midlands?" Lyons asked as they walked downstairs again.

"You bet! Mostly the US, Canada and occasionally South Africa or Australia. I was there last week," the courier said.

"Wow, sounds great. Bet the air miles clock up quickly," Lyons responded.

"We're not allowed to collect them. And anyway, last week I was Deirdre O'Dwyer, so it wouldn't be much use, I'm afraid."

Lyons said goodbye. She was completely bemused by the secret life of the secure courier and was still processing the whole encounter when she got back upstairs.

"Who's your new friend?" Hays asked.

"I haven't a clue. Today she's Angela Byrne, last week she was Deirdre O'Dwyer, so I don't know who the hell she is, and I've just given her what is potentially our strongest piece of evidence against Ciaran O'Shaughnessy!"

"Well, whoever she is, she's nicely packaged," Hays said.

"OK, tiger, you can put your eyes back in now," she said, giving him a friendly dig in the ribs.

The rest of the day passed quickly. The team busied themselves with emails and paperwork, bringing the computer system up to date with recent events. There was still no communication from Clifden.

# Chapter Thirty-four

The following day started well. Lyons took a call from the professor at Leicester University. He told her that the courier had arrived safely at around eight o'clock and that the coin was now in the laboratory being indexed and photographed before the process could begin. He hoped to be back on later with some further news.

Hays wasn't happy that Mulholland had not been in touch about the CCTV from the garage. He felt he might lose it if he called Clifden himself, so he asked Lyons to put in a call to see if they had found anything.

"Ah, good morning, Sergeant. I was just about to call you," Mulholland said when Lyons telephoned.

"Jim Dolan spent most of the afternoon yesterday looking at the CCTV. Now, just to be sure, it's a blue BMW three series, registration number zero, eight, C, nine, six, five, zero, one?"

"Yes, that's the one. Did you find it?" Lyons responded, trying hard not to sound impatient.

"Yes, we did. The time stamp showed three-twenty, but it could have been four-twenty, because Ferris says he doesn't reset the camera for summer time," Mulholland said.

"For fuck's sake, Séan. Well, at least you have him. Did he just fill up the car?"

"Yes, looks like it. And he didn't hang around."

"Do you know if he paid by card or cash, Séan?" she asked.

"Oh no, I never asked. But I'll get onto Ferris now and ask him to look at the till roll for that afternoon. That should tell us."

"Thanks, Séan, do that. And call me right back."

"Of course, I will," he said.

* * *

True to his word, Mulholland rang back in a few minutes and reported that O'Shaughnessy had spent €58.30 on fuel, and paid in cash.

"Thanks, Séan, that's great. Be sure to preserve the CCTV footage. That's evidence."

Lyons relayed the new information to Hays.

"Good, well now we have two more pieces of the jigsaw," he said.

"Two?" she asked.

"Yes. First, he lied to us. And second, we can place him in the vicinity at around the time the murder was committed. If that coin turns out to be any use to us, we may just have enough to charge him."

"Boss, I've been thinking."

"Oh-oh. Go on."

"Well, we have focussed most of our efforts on the nephew, and of course the QFA. What if it wasn't either of them? Do you think we should be pursuing other lines of enquiry as well?"

"Such as?"

"I don't know, but don't you think we should be looking at least?"

"Normally, I'd say yes. But let's look at this case," he said. "What motive other than extortion could there be? And who else would have wanted to harm the poor old devil?"

"Yes, but if this doesn't pan out, we're going to look pretty stupid."

"Don't worry about that. Firstly, I think it will pan out, and if it doesn't, it's down to me. I'm the senior officer, so I'll take what's coming."

"OK, I hear you, but obviously I don't want you to come a cropper on it," she said.

"What would you have us do?" Hays asked.

"I think we should get Eamon to open up a new line of enquiry. Spend some time out there. Talk to the neighbours, interview the nurse again, that sort of thing. What do you think?"

"It can't do any harm I suppose, even if it's just a 'cover your ass' tactic. OK then, set it up. Send him out there and get him to report back twice a day till he's done. And you'd better tell your friend Séan that we are invading his patch again, not that he'll care much."

"Right, boss. Will do."

\* \* \*

At two o'clock Lyons took a call from Professor Lattimer at Leicester University.

"Hello, Sergeant. I just thought I'd call you to let you know that Dr Kerel has finished with the two euro coin

193

that you sent us, and he has been able to get quite a good thumb print from it. Certainly good enough for our police to match up. We have to convert it from negative to positive for you, but I should be able to send it across by email in about an hour."

"That's terrific, Professor. Thank you so much, and thank Dr Kerel for us too," she said.

"Do call me James, Sergeant, and it's no trouble. We like having real cases to work on, and we don't get many euro coins in these parts."

Lyons thanked him again and when she had hung up she went straight into Hays' office to tell him the good news.

"Well, that's good anyway. Are the prints that they took in Cork in the system yet?" he said.

"I'll check now, but I'm sure they will be."

"Right, as soon as you get the image from the UK, get John onto it and let's see if we have a match!"

# Chapter Thirty-five

Hays wasn't expecting the call from Pat Dineen in Limerick quite so soon, nevertheless, he was glad to get it.

"Jesus, Pat, that was quick. Have you found anything out?" he said.

"As they say, Mick, 'the impossible we can do at once, miracles take a bit longer'. But it's a right pile you're after digging up here, mate. This guy is in well over his head. It's a wonder he still has all his limbs," Dineen reported.

"How so?"

"Well, you know the business he's in, that I.T. stuff that no one understands, right? It seems that when he gets a new contract, say, for five years to supply servers and all that stuff, there's a huge up-front cost. I'm told it can be between seventy and a hundred grand to buy and install the equipment. Then with that up-front cost, you don't make any money till year three of the contract, then it's gravy for a couple of years, and if you do it right the contract will roll over for another five years, and that's when you really start coining it."

"So, how is he funding these up-front costs? Surely you can lease this stuff?" Hays asked.

"Sometimes. But the depreciation on I.T. gear is so steep that the rates are almost impossible to meet, and you need a squeaky-clean credit history before anyone will touch it. Apparently one year old servers are worth about as much as a one year old pint of Guinness," Dineen said.

"So, where's he getting the dough?"

"Well, he owes the bank a right old wedge from the time of the financial crisis, so they won't lend him a penny till all that is cleared up. Looks like he's been pushed into the hands of the moneylenders. There's a guy called McInerney who launders a lot of drug money down here, and seemingly he likes to lend to businesses. His rates are surprisingly modest. He's more interested in getting clean money back. As long as you keep up the payments everything is fine, but if you fall behind, well that's another matter entirely."

"I can guess. Well, that certainly gives our man a motive. That's very useful, Pat. I presume all this is off the record?" Hays said.

"Need you ask? I want to keep my ten fingers, Mick."

"Well look, Pat, that's terrific information. Thanks a million, I owe you one."

"Don't worry, I'll collect at some stage. Good luck with it. Oh, and by the way, that solicitor he uses, what's his name, Murphy. He's as bent as a two pound note. The boys in Cork would love to see him come unstuck. If you can manage that, you'd be a hero."

"Jaysus, Pat, that's all I need. Thanks for the tip anyway. Needless to say, no one from Cork told us that. I'll see what I can do."

\* \* \*

Hays called Maureen Lyons into his office and relayed the new information that he had received from Limerick.

"So, if O'Shaughnessy was being pressured by McInerney for payment of past due instalments, that would explain the urgency in getting hold of the old man's shares," Hays said.

"It's beginning to fall into place at last," she said.

"Aren't you going to ask me about the fingerprints on the coin?"

"Well, Sergeant Lyons, any news on the fingerprints on the coin?" he asked, smiling.

"Yes, there is, sir," she replied.

"May I ask what the news is, Sergeant?"

"Yes, sir, you may," she said.

"Well?"

"Well what, sir?"

"For fuck's sake, what is the news on the fingerprint on the coin that we sent to the UK at enormous expense?"

"Oh that. Well it's a match for O'Shaughnessy's left thumb," she said.

"Nice one, Sergeant, nice one. What degree of certainty?" he asked.

"The prof in Leicester says about eighty-five per cent which would get them a positive ID in a UK court."

"Excellent. When you get a moment, can you get back on to him and ask him to send some case histories where this technique has been used and where it has led to a successful conviction. I'm going to brief the Super then we'll have a team briefing at, say, four-thirty."

\* \* \*

Hays was lucky to find the superintendent in his office. He explained the results that they had got back from the UK, and he outlined the conversation that he had had with Pat Dineen about their prime suspect.

"Christ, Mick, do you think that coin thing is enough to place him at the scene? All sounds a bit sci-fi to me. Is that all you've got?"

"That, and the tie wraps, and the CCTV from the garage. That's about it."

"I'm not convinced, Mick. A decent brief would drive a donkey and cart through that fingerprint evidence. Can you not get something more to put him at the scene?"

"I'll see what I can do. But we're getting case files from the UK where they have used it to get convictions. There's not much hope of getting anything more from the cottage, if you remember, it was torched," Hays said.

"So, what are you planning?"

"I want to lift him and bring him up here and charge him, boss."

"Jaysus, Mick. I'm not sure. I'd like to see some hard evidence before we do that. But it's your shout. Just remember if it all goes wrong, it could be bad for all of us."

"I'm meeting the team shortly, boss. We'll put our heads together and see what we can come up with."

"OK, do that, and let's hope for something a bit more positive."

* * *

Hays brought the team together and updated them. He also told them about the superintendent's misgivings and asked them all to rack their brains to see if they could come up with anything to get more evidence. Before the meeting finished, Lyons asked if anyone had heard from Flynn that day. Sally said that she had tried to call him on his mobile, but wherever he was, there must have been no signal, because it went straight to voicemail.

"OK, Sally, well can you try again, and leave a message for him to call in when he gets it? It wouldn't look good if we lost one of our own team out on the bog."

# Chapter Thirty-six

Maureen Lyons was at home that evening feeling a bit sorry for herself. She had eaten a frozen ready meal and was sipping a glass of rather good Chilean red wine in front of the telly with her feet up on the sofa.

The reason for her discontent was of course Inspector Mick Hays. She really wasn't sure where she stood with him, and it was getting her down. To be truthful, she didn't quite know what she wanted herself, but she knew that this wasn't it. She missed the physical contact with him. They were good together, but she couldn't figure out what it was that he wanted, or how much closer he was willing to get to her. And because of their working relationship, she knew she had to tread very carefully, or she would find herself reassigned to some backwater miles from anywhere.

Her thoughts were interrupted by her mobile phone just as she was topping up her glass. She looked at the screen hoping it was Hays, but was disappointed to see that it was Eamon Flynn calling.

"Hi Eamon. Good to hear from you. Where are you?"

"I'm in Clifden now. Jesus, Sarge, what a day! Sorry I couldn't call in earlier, but there's no damn signal out here."

"No worries, Eamon. It's fine. Did you get anything?"

"I think I did. I've been calling to every house all around the O'Shaughnessy place. Most of them are lock up and leave holiday cottages, but there's a few that are occupied all year round. There was one on the main road about half a mile closer to Clifden where an old couple are living. They told me that on the day O'Shaughnessy was killed, a man called to their house looking for directions to Paddy O'Shaughnessy's house. They said he was driving a blue car, but couldn't be specific about the make or year. They remember the day, because it was their son's birthday. He doesn't live there anymore, but they had a phone call with him in Dublin that evening."

"For fuck's sake, Eamon. That could clinch it. Did they identify Ciaran O'Shaughnessy?"

"I didn't have a photo on me, so no. But I can go back when I have one, and they say they'll give us a statement if we need it. I think they were quite taken with the excitement of it all, and of course they knew the old guy – not well, but they still knew him."

"God, that's terrific, Eamon. What do you want to do? Are you coming back in, or do you want us to send someone out with the photo tomorrow?"

"Any chance you could send someone out, Sarge? I'm staying in the Alcock and Brown tonight, and as you can see the phone works fine here."

"OK. I'll get someone out early to you. Expect them around ten, and then you can both go and hopefully get an

ID and a statement. Oh, and Eamon, keep Mulholland in the loop, won't you?"

When they had hung up, Eamon's call gave her the perfect excuse to phone Mick Hays. He always insisted on being brought up to date as soon as new information became available. When she had relayed the news that Eamon had discovered out near O'Shaughnessy's cottage, he asked her, "How are you doing, Maureen?"

"Oh, you know," she said. There was a moment's silence. "Well to be honest, I'm missing you quite a bit. Is that shocking?" she said.

"No. I'm missing you too. Would you like me to come over?" he said.

"Sounds good. Do you mind?"

"You're silly. See you soon," he said and hung up.

Maureen's next call was to Sally Fahy. She asked Sally to go into the station the following morning early and print out a photograph of Ciaran O'Shaughnessy from his LinkedIn profile, and then drive out to Clifden and meet up with Eamon Flynn at the Alcock and Brown.

"If you're lucky, he might even buy you breakfast!"

Sally was pleased to be asked to do what she thought of as real police work.

"Do you want me to stay with him while he does the ID and gets a statement?" she asked.

"Yes, please, that would be helpful. Thanks, Sally. I've got to go now. Goodnight," she said, as she heard Mick's car pulling up outside her flat.

She was feeling better already.

# Chapter Thirty-seven

When Superintendent Plunkett heard the news about what Flynn had discovered out west, he was a lot happier.

"It sounds like you should bring him in then. How are you going to play it?" Plunkett asked.

"I want him here, not in Cork. The Cork boys were a little bit careful about what they told us, especially about his solicitor. I want him out of there, and not just so he'll feel less comfortable."

"You'd better get him up here, tomorrow maybe?"

"Yes, I think we'll disturb his beauty sleep at around 6 a.m."

"I'd better give Cork a call and square it with them. Do you want him delivered, or will you go and collect him?" Plunkett asked.

"Delivered would be a lot handier for us, boss."

"Consider it done. He'll be here by nine in the morning."

\* \* \*

When Hays got back to the incident room, he was surprised to see the secure courier girl back in the room. He wandered over.

"Hello Angela, if it is 'Angela' today?"

"Oh yes, Angela today, tomorrow I'll be Samantha on my way to Australia," she said.

"Wow, what takes you there?"

"Just the usual. Evidence from the time that Irish girl was murdered on the street in Sydney. It's just a turnaround, out and straight back with whatever is in the bag."

"Crazy!" he said.

"It's a job, and somebody has to do it!"

"Do you ever get confused about who you are supposed to be?" he asked.

"Never. Can't afford to, that could be fatal in my job."

"Oh well, bon voyage, as they say." He headed for his office where Lyons joined him a few minutes later.

"What did goldilocks want?" she asked.

"She was just bringing back the coin and a few case files for us to use if we need them. She's mad, you know, totally mad."

"Yes, maybe, but she's gorgeous too," Lyons said.

Hays moved the conversation on quickly. "O'Shaughnessy will be here tomorrow at about nine. Plunkett is arranging for the Cork boys to lift him at around six in the morning from home. We'd better spend the rest of the day getting things in order. We need to be watertight on this one. I'm sure that little weasel of a lawyer will be onto every little detail."

"You leave him to me, boss. I don't think he likes gutsy women at all. I'll be able to shut him up. How do you want to play it?" she asked.

"Just the usual. It will be just you and me at first, and we should prepare ourselves for an extension to the detention period too in case he's holding out on us. Can you have a word upstairs?"

"Yes, sure. So, you don't think he'll roll over for us?"

"Who knows? But it's best to be prepared, isn't it?"

They spent the rest of the day getting all the evidence that they had accumulated filed neatly in plastic folders, and putting them in sequence. Hays wanted to keep the coin evidence till last and try to use it to trump anything the sleazy solicitor could come up with.

By the end of the day, they felt that they were as prepared as they could be, and they left the station with a sense of anticipation for the next day, wondering if they could close out the murder of Paddy O'Shaughnessy.

But the next day was one of those days that you wanted to be done with as soon as it started. It was raining heavily in Galway, and overhead, thick grey clouds showed no sign of yielding to anything better. At ten past nine Hays took a call from the squad car that had O'Shaughnessy on board. There had been a bad accident on the Gort Road, and they were delayed, now estimating arrival at around ten o'clock or soon after. Hays asked if their client had been in touch with his lawyer. He was told that he had, and that Murphy was on the road about fifteen minutes behind them.

"Let's hope he gets pinged for speeding," Hays said to the Cork Garda before letting him go.

* * *

O'Shaughnessy arrived full of bluster, claiming police harassment, and promising to lodge a stern complaint with the Garda Ombudsman over his grossly unfair treatment. He was put in an interview room to calm down, and offered coffee and water, both of which he readily accepted.

Hays had already refreshed the team on the rules of the interview. It would of course be taped, but they still had to write everything that was said down as well, and there could be no more than four Gardaí in the room at any one time. A mandatory break after four hours was also required, if it went on that long.

Twenty minutes later Daniel Murphy arrived all hot and bothered, spluttering about Garda harassment too, and his client being an important businessman with more to be doing than amusing the Gardaí, and so on.

Hays bundled him into the same interview room, telling him that he was sure the solicitor needed a few minutes to consult with his client before the interview started. They agreed to commence proceedings in fifteen minutes.

When Hays and Lyons were seated opposite the other two, Murphy began his tirade again. Lyons let him vent for about three minutes, and then cut in.

"Mr Murphy, your client is here to answer questions about the brutal torture and murder of his uncle. No amount of huff and puff on your part is going to stop us asking him the questions that we need answered, so you may as well pipe down and let us get on with it."

"You can't speak to me like that. I'm a solicitor!"

"Mr Murphy, if you persist along these lines for much longer, I will have you arrested for obstructing the Gardaí with our enquiries. Do I make myself clear?"

"I don't like your attitude one bit, Sergeant Lyons," he retorted, recognising that he had once again been defeated.

"Well, if you'd stop playing silly buggers, I might be able to change," she said, smiling at him sweetly. It was time for Hays to intervene.

"Mr O'Shaughnessy, last time we interviewed you, you said that on the day your uncle was killed, you had a business meeting in Limerick, and that when that meeting was over, you drove back to your business premises in Cork. Is that correct?"

"Yes, I have told you already," he said.

Hays saw Murphy getting ready to speak, so he put his hand up to silence him.

"So, how do you account for the fact that your car was photographed by a speed camera van travelling north towards Galway at almost 130 kilometres per hour on that afternoon?"

O'Shaughnessy didn't miss a beat. Hays thought that he might have got the fine in the post already and was therefore prepared for the question.

"There's obviously been a mistake. Those things are notoriously unreliable. I'll be contesting it. I told you, I was on my way back to Cork."

"So, just to be completely clear then, you're saying that you didn't drive north from Limerick on that day, is that correct?"

"Yes, it is," he replied.

This time Murphy couldn't contain himself.

"Sergeant," he said, addressing Hays, "my client has already answered your question a number of times, now can we move on, please?"

"It's Inspector, Mr Murphy, not Sergeant, and your client has lied to me on this issue more than once, so I'll continue with this line of questioning until I get the truth."

Hays brought out the next folder and placed it in front of the two men.

"This is a still photograph taken from CCTV footage at the petrol station in Clifden on the afternoon that your uncle was murdered. It clearly shows your vehicle, and you yourself. As you can see it is date and time stamped. You purchased fifty odd euros worth of petrol and paid in cash. Ring any bells?"

"No comment," came the reply, although O'Shaughnessy had gone noticeably paler.

Hays took the next piece of paper out of its plastic pocket, but this time, he didn't show it to the suspect, or his solicitor.

"This is a statement from a couple who live down the road from your uncle's house. In it they state that on the afternoon in question, a man who they have identified as you from your LinkedIn profile photograph, called to their house asking for directions to Paddy O'Shaughnessy's place. They say this man was driving a blue car."

"That's nonsense. They're old, and probably confused. They haven't seen so much excitement in years, so they'll say anything you tell them to say. Busy bodies!"

Lyons was onto it in a flash.

"How do you know they are old? No one said anything about their age."

"Well, everyone living out there is old, aren't they? All the young people have moved to the cities," he said, recovering somewhat.

Lyons and Hays looked at each other and an imperceptible nod went between them.

Hays produced the two euro coin, still in its little see-through plastic box that Angela Byrne had brought back from the UK.

"This is a coin that was found in the grass in front of your uncle's house after it had been burnt out by the Morrissey brothers on your instruction," Hays said, knowing he was pushing it. Murphy wasn't slow to respond.

"Now look here, Sergeant, you have absolutely no evidence that my client had anything to do with that fire, none at all. This is outrageous!"

"It's Inspector, Mr Murphy, and I have the CCTV stills that we showed you previously, where your client," he said looking directly at O'Shaughnessy, "purchased the mobile phone that was used to pass instructions to the Morrisseys."

Murphy was clearly pleased that he had managed to divert attention away from the issue of the coin.

"So, as I was saying, this coin was found in the grass outside the house. We have had it forensically tested, and that test revealed a distinct thumb print from one side of the coin. That thumb print matches exactly the print that you voluntarily gave to the Gardaí in Cork, Mr O'Shaughnessy. What have you to say to that?"

Murphy chimed in again.

"Prints from a coin. Good God, I've heard it all now. You can't get prints from a coin, man, that's impossible!

What nonsense is this? You really are desperate, Sergeant, aren't you?"

"It's Inspector, Mr Murphy."

Lyons took the moment to intervene.

"So, you are denying that you were the last person to be in possession of this coin then, Mr O'Shaughnessy?"

O'Shaughnessy just shrugged his shoulders. Murphy came back in.

"If you are going to attempt to place my client at the scene using that coin, I want to see full details of the so called forensic tests that have been carried out on it. It all seems like science fiction to me!"

Lyons then surprised them by saying, "Let's take an early lunch. I'm sure you'll want to consult with your client, Mr Murphy. We'll resume at, say, one-thirty." She tidied up the evidence folders and stood up to leave the room.

Outside the interview room she said to Hays, "Can you continue with Eamon for a while? I've got something I need to do that will take about an hour."

"Sure, no problem. Anything I should know about?"

"You'll see," she said, smiling.

* * *

When they resumed the questioning of Ciaran O'Shaughnessy at just after one-thirty, Daniel Murphy opened the discussion.

"My client would like to clarify some of the information he has previously given you, Mr Hays," he said.

"Right, go ahead, Mr O'Shaughnessy, and by the way, Mr Murphy, it's Inspector Hays."

O'Shaughnessy went on to say that on the day in question he had in fact visited his uncle in Derrygimlagh. He had gone to see if his uncle would lend him some money to save his business. He knew that Paddy had the same number of Coca Cola shares that his father had left in his will, and if Paddy could just lend them to him for a few months, he would be able to pay the money back with interest.

O'Shaughnessy insisted that his uncle had been fine when he left him. As it went, Paddy had not admitted ownership of the shares, and told him that his finances were nobody's business but his own. In any case, Paddy had told him that Ciaran would inherit whatever few bob he had when he died, and joked that that wouldn't be too long in any case.

"So, you're telling me that Paddy was perfectly fine when you departed?"

"Yes, of course. We parted amicably. He even asked me to come and visit him again soon, as he could get lonely living there on his own."

"I see," Hays said, "well that's all very well, but the fact is that he was murdered on the very same day that you visited him. And then we have the issue of the tie tags."

"What about them?" asked Murphy.

"We believe that the tie tags that were used to restrain Mr O'Shaughnessy, presumably before he was beaten senseless, are similar to ones that you use in your business," he said.

"And how would you know that?" the solicitor asked.

"Let's just say it remains to be confirmed, but I'm sure your client would have no objection to providing us with some tie wraps from his business premises for the purposes of comparison."

"Of course, if it's absolutely necessary, but I think you're grasping at straws, Sergeant."

Hays suspended the interview for a comfort break and wished he could hear what O'Shaughnessy and his solicitor were discussing in his absence. He had deliberately appeared to buy the revised story that O'Shaughnessy had dreamt up. Indeed, large parts of it were entirely true.

When Hays went back in, he advised the two that he had applied for and been granted a further twenty-four hours to question the man. Great protestation from both parties ensued, and Murphy milked it for all it was worth.

"My client has answered everything that you asked of him and we have cooperated in every way possible. This is an outrageous abuse of process. I'll be speaking to your superiors about this directly, Sergeant," he spluttered, his face getting redder by the minute.

Hays had to admit that he was enjoying Murphy's apparent distress more than he should, but he didn't show it. His response was robust.

"No, Mr Murphy. Your client has lied to us persistently until such time as we could conclusively prove that he was being untruthful. He still hasn't told us the whole story, and as I am sure you know, we are entirely within our rights to extend the time once correct procedures have been followed, which, I can assure you, they have."

"But I'll have to stay over. What time are you planning to resume the interview tomorrow morning?" Murphy asked.

"Shall we say ten o'clock? And I can promise you, Galway has some very fine lodgings and excellent restaurants, so you won't be uncomfortable for one night away from home."

* * *

Back in the incident room Hays rejoined Lyons and they both went into his office.

"This is not looking good, Maureen. He's got quite a convincing story all worked out. If only the place hadn't been burnt down, we could have got DNA from whatever he used to clobber the old guy with."

"Don't worry, boss. I have a little surprise lined up for our Mr O'Shaughnessy that I think you'll enjoy," she said with a smug smile.

"Do tell."

"All in good time, Inspector, or should I say Sergeant. All in good time."

# Chapter Thirty-eight

The interview recommenced the following morning at ten o'clock. Murphy was complaining as usual, but Hays ignored him, and Lyons just kept on giving him dirty looks. Hays focused on the meeting that O'Shaughnessy claimed to have had with his uncle.

"Can you remember exactly how the conversation went between you?" he asked.

"Well no, not exactly, but I remember the gist of it."

Hays made O'Shaughnessy repeat the account of the meeting, hoping the man would slip up or contradict himself in some way. At ten-twenty, Eamon Flynn entered the room and asked to speak to Maureen Lyons outside for a moment. A few minutes later she came back in and sat down. Hays looked at her, encouraging her to speak.

"Mr O'Shaughnessy, I have just been informed that your bank has appointed a receiver to your business, ITOS Limited. Your staff have been asked to continue with their work for the time being, but your bank accounts are now frozen, pending transfer of power of attorney to the receivers. It's been made clear that if you propose to re-enter the building, you should do so by appointment with them. The locks have been changed, and the receiver has requested the return of your BMW which is, I believe, a company asset."

A stunned silence filled the room. Colour drained from the suspect's face. The solicitor was, for once, speechless, no doubt shifting his concern to his lavish fee which must by now be in question. Neither of the two detectives uttered a word.

O'Shaughnessy's eyes filled with tears. He put his hands to his face and leant forward, supporting the weight of his head with his elbows on the table.

"Oh no, oh no," he sniffed, "I didn't mean to kill him. I just…"

"I strongly advise you not to say anything more, Mr O'Shaughnessy," Daniel Murphy interjected, putting his hand on his client's forearm.

"If he had just handed the bloody shares over. But he kept saying he didn't have them, and I was desperate, you see. McInerney had threatened me, I needed the money to save my skin."

"Really, Ciaran, please, for your own…"

"Oh shut up, Daniel. You've done enough already. Getting hold of the shares was your idea in the first place. Just shut up, will you?"

O'Shaughnessy went on to describe how he had tied Paddy to his chair using tie wraps from his car, and then searched the little house for the shares certificates. Paddy was shouting at him, calling him names, and he just lost it. He whacked him with something from the fireplace and the old man went quiet. He kept on searching the house but found nothing, and then he realized that the old man had died.

Yes, it was him in the internet café. Yes, it was him in the Meteor shop buying the pay as you go phone.

\* \* \*

When they returned to the incident room, the word had got out. Plunkett had come down from on high with a fresh bottle of Jameson Crested Ten whiskey, and congratulations were handed out all round.

"What will we do with the bent solicitor?" Hays asked.

"I'll have a word with the folks in Cork. We'll let them take care of him," Plunkett said.

"And as for you, Maureen Lyons, you little minx!" Hays said, smiling broadly.

"What? What did I do?" She smiled back.

"How did you get the bank to act so quickly?" he asked.

"Connections, sir. When my connection heard that their client was being questioned about a murder, and could be involved with moneylenders, they couldn't wait to get in there and preserve whatever assets they could get their hands on."

"Well, clearly that's what swung it. We'll make a detective out of you yet, Sergeant Lyons!" he said, putting his arm around her shoulder and clinking glasses with her.

# Chapter Thirty-nine

O'Shaughnessy was brought before the courts on the charge of murder. He was remanded in custody, as, with his business finished, he was considered a realistic flight risk. While on remand, he was severely beaten by some of McInerney's associates, as the money lender saw little prospect of recovering the substantial sums he was owed, and he needed to send out a message to his other debtors.

The receiver kept the business going, because despite the large debts, the importance of some of the contracts that ITOS had with various government departments, including some functions within the Garda Siochána itself, meant that it couldn't just be shut down. Eventually, it was sold for quite a good price to a large I.T. company, and the creditors got a substantial amount of their money back. Except for McInerney, of course.

O'Shaughnessy eventually agreed to plead guilty to manslaughter of his uncle, and as he probably didn't set out to murder him on that fateful day, the Gardaí were happy to settle for that. When he came before the courts again, he was given ten years. He was moved to Mountjoy Prison in Dublin for his own safety, but he still could not escape McInerney's contacts, and was attacked regularly by other inmates and badly beaten.

The Gardaí in Cork tried a number of different approaches to discover what part Murphy had played in the O'Shaughnessy case. But however hard they tried, they could get no hard evidence of wrong-doing. He had certainly been up to no good, but he was slippery, and had covered his tracks well. He continued to practice in Cork.

When the drug squad got hold of Kelly, they slowly uncovered a web of criminality which led them to the arrest of a whole team of dealers and pushers in the Galway area. Kelly had been using his business as a cover for drug dealing and money laundering, and eventually the drug squad discovered over 100,000 euro that they could link to him in one way or another.

He was brought before the courts and received a sentence of eight years. The house in Shantalla Road, which turned out to be his own, continued to decay, and is unoccupied to this day.

Following the success of this difficult case, Superintendent Plunkett wasted no time in exploiting the team's achievement. He put his plans to extend the major incident investigation team into practice and made the changes that he had envisaged. His idea to create the role of Senior Inspector, akin to the grade of 'Detective Chief Inspector' in Britain, caught on, and was adopted by other regions who wanted to promote and reward successful detectives. He even managed to get a supplementary allowance for the role, which created clear space between a mere inspector and the new position. He also got approval to expand Hays' team.

After the arrest, Maureen took a few days off. She spent the two bank holiday weekends that came in early May and early June over at Hays' house doing the place up with him. They got new carpets downstairs, painted all the woodwork, changed the old tired sofa in the lounge for a fresh new one, and inspired by the overhaul, Hays even ordered a new kitchen. When they had finished the house was totally transformed, and no longer had the appearance of a somewhat slovenly bachelor's pad.

Of course, Maureen wouldn't hear of taking any money for her efforts, so Hays took himself into Galway one day on the pretext of getting some more paint for the front door, went to Hartmans the jewellers, and bought her an exquisite and very expensive Rotary gold watch. She cried when he gave it to her. No one had ever been that generous to her before.

Later that year, egged on by Hays, Plunkett and the rest of the team, Maureen took her inspector's exams and passed with exceptional grades. Plunkett was able to give her the inspector's post that had been vacated when Hays was made up, and her promotion was warmly welcomed, and extensively celebrated, by the entire station. Maureen became the first female detective inspector in the western region, which marked a turning point for the force in terms of gender balance.

Eamon was promoted to detective sergeant in line with the other promotions, so he took over Maureen's place in the pecking order.

John elected to stay in uniform and felt it was too early for him to apply for promotion. He was happy to continue assisting the team with their technology. He was becoming quite a wizard with the PC and wasn't beyond a bit of discreet hacking to unlock a thorny case when the occasion demanded.

Sally applied for and was accepted into Templemore on the strength of a glowing recommendation from Hays, countersigned by the superintendent. She emerged from training looking stunning in her new uniform, and the rest of the team went to her passing out parade to help her celebrate.

When she had completed her probation, Hays asked her if she would like to join the detective unit in Galway, and she readily accepted. She became Detective Garda Sally Fahy, complete with warrant card, and wore the title with pride.

# List of Characters

Mary Drinan – the portly district nurse who is under pressure to see all her patients as frequently as their needs require but is too busy to do her job properly. Mary is a kindly person but feels exploited by the Health Authority.

Paddy O'Shaughnessy – a lonely bachelor who lives in a semi-dilapidated cottage in a remote part of Connemara. He's too old and infirm to drive any longer, so he lives in solitude, and relies on the generosity of neighbours to get into town a few times a week.

Detective Inspector Mick Hays – the senior officer in the Galway Detective Unit with many years' experience in crime detection. A confirmed bachelor, Hays is building a strong team in anticipation of an expansion of the unit in the near future.

Detective Sergeant Maureen Lyons – Hays' 'bagman' in Galway, Maureen is constantly trying to prove herself while wrestling with loneliness in her private life. A feisty, ambitious and tough woman with powerful instincts who has a knack of being in the right place at the right time.

Detective Garda Eamon Flynn – known for his tenacity, Flynn wanted to work as a detective since he was a small boy. He develops his skill while working on the case and proves invaluable handling some tricky customers.

Garda John O'Connor – the nerdy and modest junior member of the team is a technical wizard. He loves working with PC's, mobile phones, cameras and anything electronic.

Sergeant Séan Mulholland – happy to take it easy in the quiet backwater of Clifden, Mulholland could have retired by now, but enjoys the status that the job affords him. Not to be hurried, he runs the Garda Station at a gentle pace.

Garda Jim Dolan – works alongside Mulholland and has little ambition to do anything else.

Pat Dineen – a hardened Detective Inspector used to dealing with tough Limerick criminals, and a friend of Mick Hays.

Superintendent Finbar Plunkett – a wily old hand in the Garda Siochána, he knows how to play the media and the commissioner to ensure that he's allowed to do more or less what he wants in Galway. He takes a very expedient approach to problem solving.

Sally Fahy – a civilian worker with the Gardaí, Sally has aspirations to become a Garda herself, as she is fascinated by the work that she sees going on all around her but is concerned about how young women might be treated in the force.

Ciaran O'Shaughnessy – runs his own I.T. company in Cork and is Paddy O'Shaughnessy's nephew. He is a clever man, with a very deep knowledge of all matters related to computers, but isn't as smart when it comes to business acumen.

Jazz and Dingo Morrissey – two brothers from the criminal underworld who are not as clever as they think they are. These two will do anything for a few pounds as long as it's in hard cash.

Daniel Murphy – a slippery solicitor with a low opinion of the police. He is more involved than anyone knows but usually manages to wriggle out of any unpleasant consequences.

Jerome Kelly – a financial advisor that could do with taking some proper advice.

Brendan and Cathal – two firemen from the Galway fire station

Julian Dodd – the slightly superior, but highly competent pathologist attached to the Galway police. Although he is sometimes hard to take, he has helped the Gardaí enormously with his thorough forensic knowledge.

McInerney – a very rough criminal from the Limerick area who is into drugs and money lending.

Professor Lattimer – a highly qualified forensic scientist from Leicester University who works with Dr Andrew Kerel on some fascinating new techniques to identify perpetrators of crime.

Sinéad – a member of the Garda Technical Bureau with a sense of humour which comes to the fore in the darkest situations.

Neville Watson – a bank manager with a bad attitude who is frightened of his Head Office and hides behind procedure at all costs.

Angela Byrne – a pretty girl with a number of aliases who spends her time travelling the world collecting and delivering items of evidence for the Gardaí.

If you enjoyed this book, please let others know by leaving a quick review on Amazon. Also, if you spot anything untoward in the paperback, get in touch. We strive for the best quality and appreciate reader feedback.

editor@thebookfolks.com

www.thebookfolks.com

**BOOKS BY DAVID PEARSON**

*In this series:*

Murder on the Old Bog Road (Book 1)
Murder at the Old Cottage (Book 2)
Murder on the West Coast (Book 3)
Murder at the Pony Show (Book 4)
Murder on Pay Day (Book 5)
Murder in the Air (Book 6)
Murder at the Holiday Home (Book 7)
Murder on the Peninsula (Book 8)
Murder at the Races (Book 9)

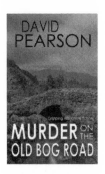

A woman is found in a ditch, murdered. As the list of suspects grows, an Irish town's dirty secrets are exposed. Detective Inspector Mick Hays and DS Maureen Lyons are called in to investigate. But getting the locals to even speak to the police will take some doing. Will they find the killer in their midst?

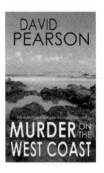

When the Irish police arrive at a road accident, little do they know it will lead to evidence of a kidnapping and a murder. Detective Maureen Lyons is in charge of the case but struggling with self-doubt, and when a suspect slips through her fingers she must act fast to save her reputation and crack the case.

A man is found dead during the annual Connemara Pony Show. Panic spreads through the event when it is discovered he was murdered. Detective Maureen Lyons leads the investigation. But questioning the local bigwigs involved ruffles feathers and the powers that be threaten to stonewall the inquiry.

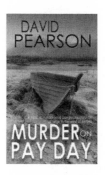

Following a tip-off, Irish police lie in wait for a robbery. But the criminals cleverly evade their grasp. Meanwhile, a body is found beneath a cliff. DCI Mick Hays' chances of promotion will be blown unless he sorts out the mess.

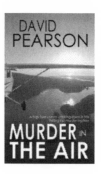

After a wealthy businessman's plane crashes into bogland it is discovered the engine was tampered with. But who out of the three occupants was the intended target? DI Maureen Lyons leads the investigation, which points to shady dealings and an even darker crime.

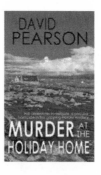

A local businessman is questioned when a young woman is found dead in his property. His caginess makes him a prime suspect in what is now a murder inquiry. But with no clear motive and no evidence, detectives will have a hard task proving their case. They'll have to follow the money, even if it leads them into danger.

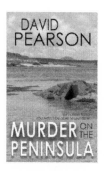

When a body is found in a car on a remote beach, detectives suspect foul play. Their investigation leads them to believe the death is connected to corruption in local government. But rather than have to hunt down the killer, he approaches them. With one idea in mind: revenge. Working out against whom and why will be key to stopping him in his tracks.

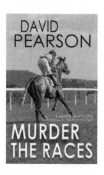

One of the highlights of Ireland's horseracing calendar is marred when a successful bookmaker is robbed and killed in the restrooms. DI Maureen Lyons investigates but is not banking on a troublemaker emerging from within the police ranks. Her team will have to deal with the shenanigans and catch a killer.

Made in the USA
Columbia, SC
18 January 2020